SACRIFICE OF MINE

JANEAL FALOR

Sacrifice of Mine

Book Four
by
Janeal Falor

To learn more about this author, please visit:
www.janealfalor.com

Cover by Rainbow Danger Designs

For My Readers
For having the courage to tell your own story

Bethany

CHAPTER 1

It's time to run. I just don't know if we'll ever be able to run fast enough or far enough to escape the Grand Chancellor. Any moment now, the law officers may find our cave, and we will be captured. After being defeated so thoroughly by the Grand Chancellor yesterday, it's a humiliating dash toward Envado. What's worse is, when we get there, we'll have to tell them Chadwick is dead, Tawny is missing, and Zade is still captured.

Waverly is understandably upset about it all, but she loses control so much whenever we mention Tawny's name, I wonder if there's more going on than we heard before. She has kept herself together better with Zade's capture than Tawny's, and he's her brother. Perhaps it's the uncertainty of Tawny's situation that's sent Waverly over the edge. What we know is she's missing, but she may be gone forever.

Waverly and Jack are sweet together, working side by side to clear as many people from the area as possible before the law officers come. It could be any time now. No one really knows. Which is why my family—all my sisters, my brother, and my mother—are leaving, even though there are still people who need assistance getting out. Waverly told the people to leave their things behind, but they can't seem to manage to, which means we can no longer stay to help.

Poor Waverly. She's trying so desperately to keep everyone together, herself included. She's doing a sad job of it, though. Ever since the battle we lost so thoroughly, she's barely holding herself together.

Lukas helps Cynthia bring my last sister out to the mouth of the cave and then takes her hand. The loving gesture isn't lost on me. Not now, when so much has been taken from us. It's also not lost on my oldest sister, Serena. As I move to her, I think about Zade's capture and our failed attempt to rescue him and the others imprisoned in the Grand Chancellor's dungeon.

A chill passes through me. What happened to the Grand Chancellor's son, Nathaniel, after his father threw him back into the house with a spell? Is he in the dungeon or somewhere worse?

I stand by Serena, wishing there was more I could do to comfort her. No matter what, I can't bring back her fiancé.

"We're not giving up on him," I say.

"I know." She sounds sad and small.

"Yet?"

"Yet we've failed him. I'll never give up, but there's no way we can ever free him from the Grand Chancellor. Not after all we've already tried to do."

"Maybe someday we'll figure something out."

"*Someday. Something.* More like no day and nothing. The Grand Chancellor is an impossible foe."

He *is* impossible to beat. Years of stealing magic from women has made him the strongest person around by a long, long way. Just thinking about him and what he can do makes my hands shake, so I force myself to think of something else.

Waverly hasn't come back to give us the go-ahead yet, but I feel uneasy about waiting any longer. "We should get going."

Serena nods, features etched with sorrow. "Gather them up."

I move to the back, making sure the girls old enough are

helping a younger girl and each girl has a buddy that will be a traveling companion until we reach Envado, however long it takes us. If we can reach it before being caught, that is. When I reach the back of the group, I grab baby Abigail from mother and take Molly by the hand.

"Let's go, sweetie."

"Where we go?" she says.

"For a long walk." Much too long a walk, especially with all these little ones. How are we going to make it to Envado with so many children? There isn't a choice, though. We have to make it.

Serena waits for us at the mouth of the cave, peeking outside to see if the law officers have reached us yet. Not that it will do any good. If they find us, we have nowhere else to run. No way out of the network of caves that's been our home.

Others are packing up to go as well, though most everyone left immediately after we lost the battle. Those who weren't captured or killed. It's hard to think of that night. Of so many dying, like Chadwick who did so to save Waverly's life. Of Nathaniel, standing up to his father. He tried so hard to help, and it just got him in bigger trouble. It makes my heart hurt to consider the possibilities.

"How long is this walk going to take?" Sally asks.

"At least a week, I think. Maybe more," I tell her, trying not to think of how grown up she sounds.

Cynthia storms into the cave. "We have to leave. Now. They're getting close."

I usher the girls and mother outside and follow the last of them, Sally. Abby is light in my arms but heavy in my heart. What type of world is she going to grow up in, now that everything else has failed?

It doesn't matter. We'll make it out of here without getting caught, and we'll go to Envado where both she and her twin brother, Benjamin, can age in a better world than I did. We were stupid not to send them there before we waged this war. Now it's an even more dangerous journey. I can only hope none of us get caught on the way.

"Do you need me to take her?" Serena asks, as we both head out of the cave.

"I'm fine. Go help get us out of here."

She nods and hurries toward the front of the group, gun in hand.

Others leave the cave after us. Too many people wanted to take their possessions with them. We said we would help those who insisted. But if the law officers are close, how many of those we spent so much time with will be caught?

I can't think of that either. We've delayed this long to help as many as we could. We can't wait any longer. Cynthia and Lukas lead the group. Jack is in the middle, carrying Molly on his shoulders. Serena moves through us, encouraging everyone on. Waverly's not in sight. She scouts the way ahead for us.

Suddenly, she bursts through the group of trees ahead of us. "Run!" Though her voice is only loud enough to carry to us, it's urgent.

Serena picks up my younger sister, Stella, and Jack grabs Ruthie, so he's now carrying two. I run with Sally at my side. She trips. The others don't notice as I stop to help her up. She puts her hand in mine, and something slaps me on the back, freezing my legs in place.

A law officer. He cast a partial freezing spell on me.

"Go," I yell at Sally.

She hesitates.

"Go now, or I'll give you a year's worth of chores." Please, please listen!

Finally, she runs. I'm sure she'll tell the others what happened. If she makes it to them. She has to make it to them. I have to distract the law officer long enough.

The law officer shoots a blue spell streaked with white sparks toward her, like the one on my legs. I block it with a red, heated

4

shield-spell. The freezing spell smashes against it and dissolves. Sally disappears into the forest, out of sight.

I shoot the same heat spell at my legs, but instead of turning it into a shield, I send pure heat. The spell blasts from me, arcing in red toward my lower half. It slams against my frozen legs and dissolves the spell around them.

I throw another heat shield up behind me as I run toward the same trees Sally disappeared into. I stretch my legs out as far as I can to cover as much distance as possible. It's not enough.

Another freezing spell hits me from behind. When I glance back, there's no longer a heat shield in place. I move to cast one more heat spell toward my feet, but it's too late. A third freezing spell slams in my shoulder and moves toward the rest of my body.

The law officer runs toward me, a second following him. I imagine the heat spell coming out of my chest and warming my entire body. The spell works as soon as I release it, letting me move again.

The law officers are too close. I'll never escape. I'll have to be satisfied with buying the others more time. I just wish someone else carried Abby. At least she's tucked safely in one of my arms. No time to think of her, though. I blast out a heat shield, so they can't freeze me again, followed by two freezing spells of my own that I let slip through the heat shield.

One law officer easily blocks the spell. The other gets hit in the chest. I focus on the free one and think of a sleep spell. That'll be more effective. I shoot it out just before he reaches my heat shield. It slams into him full force, just as he breaks through my shield.

He falls to the ground.

I focus on the second law officer, who is now free and shooting a new spell at me. I block the yellow spell with a steely-gray shield and hurl a sleep spell at him. When he manages to block it, I hurl three more. The first one misses, but the second hits him square on the forehead. He lands flat on the ground.

I did it. All that training and practicing paid off. I beat off two law officers by myself, with a baby in my arms. Women are anything but useless.

I turn and head for the trees. Before I make it two steps, another freezing spell stops me in my tracks. I glance up. I'm almost surrounded by warlocks. I flash as many sleep spells as I can at them, but they're no use. The warlocks have their own shields and there are way too many of them for me to fight off.

I'm stuck. For good this time. I don't know any way to get out of this before they reach me. Instinct tells me not to call out for help, even though Cynthia could break through this spell. Not only does she need to protect the others, but also, with two dozen law officers in sight and moving closer, even she would be hard pressed to get out of this situation.

It doesn't matter what I do. Abby and I are captured.

CHAPTER 2

The law officer in charge of the two of us isn't gentle. His spells are rough and forceful, often hurting my back as he pushes us forward. He rides behind us and has been for at least an hour. My legs are beginning to ache with the treatment. Thankfully, I'm taking the brunt of the punishment because I keep Abby safely tucked away in front of me. That presents a different problem, though.

Despite the baby's light weight, my arms burn from carrying her. Going this long without some sort of break or something to prop my arm up is not what I'm accustomed to.

Still, we walk on for what seems like hours. Who knows how long it really is? Abby starts to fuss. I bounce her in my arms, wishing I had something to feed her. She eventually falls to sleep, and I wish I could do the same. Anything to get me out of this nightmare.

A hex slams into my back with shocking force. I trip forward and catch myself with one hand, protecting Abby with the other. My wrist screams with pain.

I scramble to my feet as quickly as I can, trying to ignore the throbbing in my wrist.

"I'd go a lot faster if you'd stop hexing me." The words are out before I can stop them.

He climbs off his horse and moves right in front of me. I wrap Abby tightly in my arms.

"You dare speak to me?" he asks.

I straighten my back, pulling myself up to my full height. I'm not stupid enough to respond, but I'm also not willing to let him think he's breaking me. Even if he is.

He stares me down, his nostrils flaring. It takes everything in me not to respond, not to back down or look away. Finally —*finally*—he blinks. He shoves me on the shoulder, though thankfully not hard enough to make me fall to the ground.

"Get moving," he says.

Before he jumps back on his horse, I walk almost at a run, wishing I could get away. Where is he taking me, and what are they going to do to me once there?

My words must have done some good, though. He only hexes me once more before we come to our destination sometime later. When we reach a building that looks no different from the others except for the lack of windows, the law officer gets off his horse and prods me inside. The room is lit by the flicker of electric lights. Knowing they use people and their magic to gain electricity makes my stomach churn.

Besides the electric lights and a few chairs, there's nothing but more warlocks inside, though not a single other law officer. Who are all these people, and why am I here? What are they going to do to me? The law officer leading me stops in front of a thin gangly man with a chilling smirk.

"This one goes to the Grand Chancellor's house when you're done. Baby, too," the law officer says.

"It will be taken care of."

The law officer moves from the building without another word, leaving me alone with this smirking man who makes me shiver. The man takes a step closer, and I press the baby closer while taking a step back.

"The baby will have to wait here."

"No," I say. There's not a chance I'm leaving her behind when I've come so far with her. We may be going to the Grand Chancellor's together, but anything could happen if we're separated in the meantime.

"Do you know where you are?"

I glance around the windowless room again, trying to figure out what I've missed. Why wouldn't there be windows in a building so full of warlocks?

"I didn't think so," he says. "You can always tell the ones who aren't prepared for what's to come. Let me enlighten you. Perhaps you've heard of me. I'm a depraver."

I clench my teeth together to keep from gasping. A depraver? This can only mean one thing.

I'm about to be tarnished.

CHAPTER 3

"Set the baby down," the depraver says.

The only thing I want less than to leave her alone is to bring her with me. I can't risk subjecting her to whatever it is they're going to do to me. I glance at the exit.

"Go ahead and try it," the depraver says. "I like when they run."

He could be saying that just so I don't, but judging by the look on his face, he means it. I kiss Abby on the forehead and look for a place to set her. Nothing is good. She's just as likely to get stepped on as not, with all the warlocks milling about. There are a dozen or so of them, some doing paperwork, some chatting. All give me the creeps.

"Hurry it up."

Fine. I go to the corner of the room, hoping this will be safe enough from stray feet, and put her down. I'd put her on a desk or chair, but I'm afraid she'd roll off since she's started doing that lately. I wish I could trust someone to look after her, but being with a bunch of depravers leaves me hopeless. She looks at me, screwing up her face like she's going to cry.

"Hush now," I whisper, knowing she doesn't understand but

hoping she listens anyway. "This is the last place you want to cry. Please be a good baby until I get back."

Will she even recognize me when they're finished? Will I recognize me? There hasn't been time to think about what's to happen. I don't want to think of it. Everything moves too fast, but there's nothing I can do to stop it. Nothing I can do to change what's going to happen. I truly believe, if I tried to run, the depraver would enjoy whatever fate he'd leave me with. If I cast a spell, he can still overpower me, and I have Abby to worry about.

Besides, there are too many warlocks here for me to do anything. At least Abby seems content now as she sucks on her fist. I can only hope she stays this way until my return.

"Move it," the depraver says.

I hurry away from the baby, not wanting the depraver to transfer his wrath to her. He motions for me to go down a hall. When I hesitate, he casts an orange spell that shoves me forward. Not more of that again.

I move ahead, each step forcing more fear into my soul. The hall is bland, long, and empty, but with doors littered about. There's something eerie about them. Something that makes my skin crawl. By the time we stop at a room at the end of the hall, I'm ready to scream from all the dread soaking my entire being.

"Get in."

I'd much rather run back to Abby and fight my way out of this place. But that'd only lead to worse trouble than I've already got myself into. How did I get here in the first place? Tripping. That's right—Sally tripped, and I stopped to help her.

Well, I wouldn't change that for anything. Not if she's safe, which I have no way of knowing other than I haven't seen any of the others around. If becoming tarnished is what I get for helping my sister, I'll take it.

As I walk into the room, I can't help but think of what's to come. The tattoos on my face, I think I'll live with. Being bald isn't something I want, but it's not the worst thing either. But being spelled to be barren? To never have any children? I love my sisters so much. I always hoped one day I'd have a child of my own that I could raise in a world better than this one.

It will never happen.

I take a step back. Another spell slams into my back with searing pain. I cry out, unable to stop the sound.

"You want to run, after all," the depraver says. "I so hoped you would. By all means, keep going."

Instead of continuing my retreat, I turn and face him, putting all the determination I can muster into my gaze. They may be stripping me down to what they consider less than a person, but I will not let them take away my heart.

He snorts like a disappointed bull, and zaps another hex at me. I collapse to the floor as pain covers my entire body, like needles stabbing into me. It only lasts a brief moment but long enough for me to know deciding not to run was a good choice indeed. My whole being feels sliced, even after the spell is gone.

"Stand up."

When I don't do so immediately because of how bad the pain still is he hexes me again. A whimper of anguish escapes, but I won't allow anything more. Instead, I force myself to my feet, unwilling to give him an excuse to hex me again.

"Wait here." He grins. "Or don't. I'd love for you to see what happens if you leave this room."

With that, he's gone. My thoughts are everywhere. From Sally tripping to fighting and Abby, to hexes and depravers. They fly everywhere, making it hard to concentrate on just one thing until I look at the door. The unguarded door.

Leaving is so very tempting, but I know he'll make good on the threat, so I force myself to stay here in the middle of the room. The area is void of everything except a pathetic-looking bed. One I keep far from. Screams echo through the halls to the room every couple of minutes. They're enough to make me want to run, but I know I can't.

What exactly causes these screams? Will I be left screaming by what's to come? I don't want to think of it—don't want it to be a part of my future—but I know the thought is in vain. This is my future now, come what may.

After several minutes, there are footsteps. I can't help but shake for fear of what's to come. Of what's causing the screaming. The footsteps belong to a woman. Not tarnished, just a Chardonian woman with a vicious smile on her face. She's holding scissors to prepare me to be bald the rest of my life, no doubt. Why would she agree to help with this? It probably is that she has no choice, but even then, I can't imagine doing this to others. And if she has no choice, why is she smiling like that?

I force myself to be brave enough to ask, "Why are you doing this?"

"So I don't have to become one of you." She lifts her scissors toward me.

This feels nothing like when Cynthia cut her own hair. Panic rises within me. They can't do this. They can't just take my hair. They can't make me into something I'm not. My stomach churns. Despite the earlier punishment, I try to back away. Her hand grabs me and holds me still.

"Don't fight it. There's nothing you can do to stop it," the woman says.

As true as those words may be, they don't make me feel any better. "You don't have to do this."

"Of course I do. You think I have any more of a choice than you do?"

"I think you like the power it gives you over others."

She smiles again before reaching forward and grabbing a handful of hair. Soon my locks are falling, falling, falling to the ground. Hair I took years to grow, gone within a matter of moments. The strands look so desolate, lying on the ground by themselves. I don't want her to cut more. I want to control it myself, at the very least, but I've never had full control over anything in my life, and this is even worse. I have control over nothing.

As the locks continue to fall, I can't decide which is stronger—the urge to scream or that to rip the scissors out of the woman's hands and chop off her hair like she has done so unabashedly to mine.

I do neither. Just stand there as I lose my hair. When it's all chopped close to my scalp, the woman calls out, "She's ready for you."

I shiver at the words. The depraver who taunted me before enters the room. Fear coils within me. I know whatever comes next, I'm not going to like. He stares at me curiously. Not even with disdain like warlocks have looked at me my entire life, but like… like I'm not even a person. Like I'm some sort of thing he finds pleasure in toying with.

I clench my teeth harder, unwilling to let my true feelings show. Fear and hatred boil within me. I suppose to him I'm no longer what little of a person I was once considered. I'm little meant to become less. To be tarnished.

He chortles, and the glee in the sound abounds through the room and makes me curl in on myself. He casts a black spell with yellow swirling through it. It moves straight toward my head. The last of my hair falls from my head in one chilling swoop.

I reach up and touch the smoothness he's uncovered. Nothing. Not even a single strand remains. Why would they do this to me or anyone else? What are they trying to make happen by getting rid of our hair? Why do they find enjoyment in tarnishing people?

I know why. They're crazy and enjoy hurting women. I take deep, slow breaths to keep from crying. I'm losing my humanity. After this, I'll be less than a person. Less than a shadow. Less than anything.

And he's not finished. He clamps his fingers around my face

and forces it first to one side and then the other. He digs his fingers into my skin, leaving it aching with pain. I try to pull away, but it only hurts more, so I stop struggling. He gives no sign or acknowledgment that I even tried. Just continues to leer at me, his creepy grin growing.

He holds up a single finger from his free hand and traces across my face several inches away from it. Black with bright purple swirls out, tracing across my skin. I can't figure out what exactly he's doing. Is this how he'll leave me tattooed with the marks I will carry the rest of my life? I thought it would hurt more. It takes a while to go across my whole face, making who knows what pattern on it.

Finally, he lets go. "You want to hold still for this next part."

I don't have time to fully comprehend the sense of foreboding his words bring before the pain screams across my face. The spell he traced leaves me aching. I want to shriek, but that would be moving. I concentrate as hard as I can on staying still, but the pain is dark and gruesome.

At first, all I can do is focus on the pain. Gradually, my sisters come to mind. Their sweetness and goodness. The way they always love me. Bring joy to my life. And mother, coming to show her kindness more recently. Being away from my father's rule has made her open up. Show her love and sweetness.

Then Nathaniel comes into my thoughts. Why him, I'm uncertain, but thoughts of him are a soothing balm against the screeching pain scorching my skin.

After an interminable amount of time, the spell *finally* stops. My face is searing. All I want is something cool and soothing against my skin, to ease the pain burning me. But I don't dare try a spell with him watching me, and there's nothing else to use.

The pain throbs, making me dizzy. I collapse to the ground, and my face slams against the floor. All goes black.

* * *

I WAKE, my face tender, my lower stomach aching. My head is groggy as I try to remember where I am and why I'm in such pain. Then it all comes back to me. Worse yet, I remember why the pain is there.

I'm now barren.

I roll onto my back on the cold floor. Clothes scrape against my skin. Clothes that aren't mine. A brown skirt and tan shirt are on me. Definitely not mine, but I guess they're about the only thing I will be wearing from now on.

Everything is hazy. A strange mix of pain and haziness. Until I remember Abby. My thoughts clear with startling brightness. I have to go to her. Pushing through the pain, I press my back against the nearest wall and hope it will give me strength to stand. The depraver enters the room.

"Ah, you're awake. Good. It's time for you to go to your new home." He turns toward another warlock, who entered behind him. "See that she gets to the Grand Chancellor's, along with the baby she came with. He's expecting them both."

"Of course." As soon as the depraver is gone, the other warlock says, "Get up."

I want to do nothing of the sort now he's here. I want to curl into a ball and hide. I never want to come out again. I'm bald, my face aches, and my stomach is on fire, meaning I'll never have children again. My face is inked. Worst of all, I've become nothing. I'm no longer human.

The only thing that gets me moving is the thought of Abby. I'm not sure what it could possibly mean that the Grand Chancellor is expecting her as well. Whatever it is, I'll have to do better protecting her than I've done protecting myself. I don't know how it's possible, but I'll do everything in my power to make certain no one hurts her.

I follow the warlock back to the room I first entered and find Abby fast asleep, though she smells rather ripe. No nappies available. It will just have to wait.

The warlock leads us through the building out to a window-less carriage and shoves me inside. I roll so Abby doesn't hit the floor. My shoulder jams into the wooden bench, adding one more injury to my aching body. The door shuts, leaving the baby on the floor alone, with me tarnished.

CHAPTER 4

We don't travel very far before the carriage pulls over. The smell is something awful due to the unchanged nappy. They had better have something to help me rectify this as soon as possible. Poor Abby has to be miserable. My nose certainly is.

The door opens.

"Out with you," an unfamiliar man says.

I comply, ready to face my fate and not wanting to stay in this thing any longer. My pain has lessened, but I'm still achy. The baby wakes in my arms but stays quiet as I bounce her on the walk toward the Grand Chancellor's house. She's such a good little thing.

The house has no evidence of our fight. It fills me with despair to think nothing we fought for remains. Not even scars of our war. Just a mansion filled with people to do the Grand Chancellor's bidding.

I can't help but wonder if Nathaniel is in here somewhere. After he was flung back into the house during the fight, I'm not certain what happened to him. I don't know whether I hope he's here or not. There's so much damage his father can do. It may be better if he's not here at all. But then, if he's not here, where else would his father send him? Might it be some place even worse than this? Would he send him to the dungeons or a power plant? I hate to think of it.

We go in through a side door and wind through lavish hallways. Gold covers everything. What little isn't gold is a deep, dark wood. Pictures of landscapes and mirrors line the walls. Every few feet I see a golden stand holding a potted plant. Everything is immaculate.

We continue on until we come to a grand sitting room, the occupants of which make me want to go running back to the depravers.

The Grand Chancellor and Father.

Father's bulky frame takes up more than just his chair. Seeing him again makes me want to cringe. To hide or make excuses. Instead, I clench my teeth and hold the baby closer to me despite her foul diaper.

"Finally here," the Grand Chancellor says. "Stephen has been anxious to meet his son. Bring him here."

Son? They think Abby is her twin brother, Benjamin? Merciful master. How am I to explain it's not him? What punishment will befall me because of it? I don't think they can do worse to me than they've already done, but it doesn't mean it won't hurt.

But wait.

I don't have to tell them anything. They never have to know. Unless father suddenly decides to change her nappy, how will he know I'm carrying his sixteenth daughter?

A worse thought hits me. If father is here and thinks this is his son, are we to be parted? And if so, what will happen when whoever takes care of the babe next realizes this is Stephen's daughter and not his son?

I mince forward to the last place I want to be. The last person I want to turn Abby over to. Father snatches her out of my hands when I reach him. I clench my jaw and hover protectively.

"My son," he exclaims and then scrunches his face. "Smells foul."

He shoves her back at me, and I grab onto her like to a lifeline.

"Would you like a nurse for him?" the Grand Chancellor asks. "I can have one brought in."

Brought in? Dare I hope this means she'll be staying in this house? Has father found no other place to live since we burnt down his place? A small bit of satisfaction fills me.

"Don't trouble yourself. His sister…" He squints at me. "Which one are you? Never mind. It doesn't matter. She can look after him. All my older girls have experience with babies. More than most nurses you'll find. When he's old enough to learn, I'll get him a proper setting with a tutor."

Can it be? Can father be leaving me in charge of Abby? My heart soars for the first time since we were captured. I'll be able to hide the fact that she's a girl. I'm uncertain how long I'll be able to do so, but for a time I'll save her from being sent away. Or worse. I shudder.

"This tarnished can bring him to you whenever you like," the Grand Chancellor says. "The others will show her where your wing is. I do have something I'd like to do to her, if you're amiable."

I hold my breath, fearing what it could possibly be.

"What is that?" my father asks. They discuss me like I'm not even present. Or worse, like I'm less than an object they'd take notice of.

"As you know, at the coming tournament, I will be killing the Envadi and his rebel friend. I think it would be a nice addition if I was to sacrifice this tarnished first, proving not only are male rebels dealt with, but even the girl of a chancellor."

My stomach roils. He means Zade and Daniel. I'm to be killed alongside them.

"By all means, you may do whatever you please with her. I can get a new nurse then."

I want to vomit on them both. They speak of my imminent death as if it were nothing more than what they'll have for breakfast. The threat of death is nothing new to me, though. As long as I tell myself it's only a threat, I'll manage not to fall apart, because falling apart is the last thing I can do right now. I have Abby to look after.

"Good," the Grand Chancellor says. "Will you mark her for me as the sacrifice for the tournament?"

Mark me? Again? How much more can they mark me up?

"Certainly." To me he says, in a rougher voice, "Over here, girl."

My legs don't want to move. They don't want to do anything at all. Somehow, I force them forward. This isn't going to be as bad as the depraver's spell. At least that's what I tell myself.

Father casts a spell of bright yellow and with it makes a slash motion across my neck. Nothing feels any different, but I'm sure I'm to be. There's no way to get out of this if I'm marked in such a way.

The Grand Chancellor turns to another tarnished I hadn't noticed, who stands in the corner. This makes me realize many of them are scattered through the room in the most discrete locations.

"Take her away," he says, "and make certain she knows the rules."

The tarnished nods. I need no prompting to hurry after her. She leads me through the house not showing me anything, as silent as all the other tarnished I met before Katherine came along. Just thinking her name makes me miss Katherine. I wish I asked her more about what happened when she became tarnished. How she ended up running her own dress shop. Not that she is now. Not after Zade was imprisoned.

Zade. I'm in the very house he's in. Somewhere below me is a dungeon in which he's held prisoner with Daniel, Annabelle's husband, and perhaps others who were captured in the final battle. Maybe, just maybe, I'll be able to collect information on them and spell it out to Serena. Though mail spells aren't my best. I can never seem to get them quite right, but I'll practice. I'll practice and hope I can find some information to share. Good information, that is. Please let them be well.

The tarnished takes me to a laundry room currently empty of any other people. It's heavy with unfound dreams and dank with lost hope.

It almost makes me want to lie down and never get back up. There's been too much pain and hardship everywhere we turn. I cannot handle it any longer. At least we're away from the warlocks who make our life the misery it is, though still under the same roof.

The tarnished woman says, "I figured this would be as good a place as any to talk, since no one is here and that little one needs a new nappy."

She goes to a pile of rags and hands me a large amount. "This should be enough to last a while. Let me do some washing, while you tell me how you came to be here." She hurries over to a bin and starts scrubbing clothes.

"The Grand Chancellor has electricity," I say. "I thought he'd have electric washers."

"Not for us." She seems to choose her words carefully. "He prefers the electricity for him and his guests."

In other words, it doesn't matter what people who are less than shadows do—or do without. I'm now one of these people. How long will it take me to get used to the fact I'm now tarnished?

This gives me the opportunity to change Abby's nappy without revealing she's a girl. I don't know what my responsibilities here will be, but it already seems difficult to keep her gender a secret.

I turn my back to the woman helping me, and hurry to take care of Abby's mess while telling the tarnished how we were captured trying to escape the country. The words leave my heart torn and aching. I hope the others made it. They have to be safe. Otherwise my not calling out was for naught.

"First thing you must know," she says, "is we can't leave the grounds. We die instantly if we do."

There's a spell that can do that? It's not one I'm willing to test.

At least not yet.

"The second thing is a new one. Due to the newfound magic among women, no magic is to be seen from tarnished. If you are caught doing magic, the Grand Chancellor will instantly sacrifice you. Furthermore, spells can't leave the grounds."

Fear permeates me. Everything I am has already been taken away. Do they have to take my magic too? I should have expected it, but I've become so used to it being part of my life, it didn't cross my mind. I'll never be able to spell out a message to my sisters and Waverly.

I give myself a moment to digest the new information as I finish cleaning Abby up. Once the baby's nappy is fresh, I turn to help the tarnished with the laundry. "What's your name?"

"In this house, we have no names."

Nothing is mine anymore. Not even my own name.

CHAPTER 5

The tarnished who is as nameless as I am shows me around the house and to my many duties. A house this giant needs constant attention to stay up to the Grand Chancellor's standards. Each room comes with a single word, such as *"Library"* or *"Study"* and the understanding I'll have to help with them all.

"You have cleaned before, haven't you?"

"I took care of the children mainly, but I did some cleaning as well."

She nods. "You'll fit right in, then."

That's not at all what I want to hear, but at least I won't get punishments for not fitting in. We go down a dark hall and stop at an open doorway.

"This is our room," she whispers. The room is full of over forty beds, a third of them with occupants. "It's not so bad since we sleep in shifts. Though we're only allowed five hours of sleep. You'll have to try and keep the baby quiet while you're in here or the others will be upset. In fact, you need to keep him quiet all the time. The Grand Chancellor won't want a crying baby to be heard in this house, no matter whose son he is."

How am I ever to manage? Babies just cry; it's what they do. "I'll do my best."

"You may have to do more than your best if you want to survive around here."

I swallow past the sudden thickening in my throat. "Of course."

She nods. "We have one change of clothes. If you want anything else, you'll have to buy it."

"With what money?"

She shrugs. "We all just have one change of clothes."

Back to my days with father. I had more clothes then, but not many. I would have gotten more, were I of age to be sold to a warlock. Things to show me off in. Father would parade me around, especially if my magic didn't rate high enough to attract as much attention, and I would be given to the highest bidder. I'd rather have just a change of clothes.

And then I realize it really will be back to my days with father. He's here. He'll want to see the baby, especially if he thinks she's his son. Of course, with his dismissive attitude earlier, perhaps being a tarnished around him will be better than being a daughter. No beatings or hexes, just orders. If that. Seems like tarnished around here are spoken to as little as possible. This is my life now. At least until I'm executed.

The woman who met me when I arrived lets me finish looking around then takes me through the rest of the house we didn't see before, showing me where my chores will be for the first day and explaining how to do them. What's the point of having so much space? There's more here than a person can enjoy in a day.

As we go through the process, we come across many other tarnished at work.

"This is the new girl," the woman leading me around says, and that's where introductions end, though she does eye my neck with something like pity.

By the time the tour is over, I'm exhausted just from moving through the entire house, and soon I'll have to not just move through it, but scrub it down. It's not a job for the weak, by any means.

After the tour is over, I'm given leave to sleep. I don't think I'll be able to; the weight of the day will press on my mind too much. And it does, but in the form of nightmares and fitful sleep. I wake, wondering if my five hours are up yet. Without any way to know, I take Abby and head down to the kitchen, to find her something to eat. They'll have to have some substitute for mother's milk.

I only take one wrong turn and figure it out right away. Once in the kitchen, I find several tarnished eating at a large table. If it weren't for Abby, I would grab a bowl and sit down next to them. I never did get food yesterday. I don't remember when I last ate. My stomach churns in protest.

I move over to the male tarnished at the stove. "Is there any milk I could have to feed the baby?"

"There's some goat's milk we can give him." He moves to the ice box. "Was hoping you'd stop by, so I could see the little guy. We don't get many babies around these parts."

I shift so the baby is closer to him. He coos down at her better than any other male I've seen. Maybe tarnished know more about raising babies than most others do?

He pours me a cup of the goat's milk. Not ideal, but I suppose I'll have to make it work.

"Thank you," I say.

"You just go right to the ice box any time you need to feed him."

"I will. Thank you."

I feed Abby and then start in on a bowl of mush. It's probably one of the grossest things I've ever eaten, but after being so hungry, it's a welcome relief. I glance around me as I eat. There's a lot of tarnished here. The woman that first helped me when I came here is near. The girl across from me has tattoo's that look almost like a cat's with streaks starting near her nose and moving out across her face.

There are so many others, but they start to blend together. Everyone here is another face of what the Grand Chancellor has done. What he is. Why has he done this to so many people?

I'm not halfway finished when a lower-class male servant with dirty blonde hair comes in the room and says, "To work."

The others jump up from their chairs and take their bowls to the sink. I hesitate, trying to get one more bite in.

"Get up," the servant yells at me. "That you're new doesn't excuse you. No lunch for you today. It's time for chores."

This has to be some bad joke. I jump up and hurry my bowl over to the sink, trying not to think of all the food going to waste. The cook gives me a sympathetic smile as he takes over cleaning the dishes.

The lower-class male glares at me. His eyes are sandy brown. "Let's get things straight. I'm Fredrick, and I don't tolerate laziness in tarnished. This is your one and only warning."

I lower my head like I'm bowing to his wishes, but I'm simmering inside. Well, and a little afraid. Would they really kill me before the tournament? I have to take care of Abby, so I can't chance finding out.

The woman who showed me around yesterday appears out of nowhere. "You'll be with me today. I'll make sure you know what you're doing."

I'd say thank you, but with the angry servant still watching on, I don't dare say anything at all. I follow the woman around the house and get to work, quickly falling into a rhythm. The day is long and exhausting, especially when the woman helping me breaks for lunch, and I have to keep dusting the study.

My stomach growls loudly. I wish I was quicker with my bowl this morning. One extra bite was not worth missing an entire meal.

The woman comes back, and we work, with baby in hand, on a

bedroom with attached bathroom—a flushable toilet and running water both. I can't imagine what it's like having such luxuries all the time. And of course, even though I'm in a house with them, I won't be using them so I'll have to continue wondering. They are easier to clean, at the very least.

"I'm sorry I'm not better at helping," I say. "It's hard with one hand."

"And that extra weight, I would imagine."

"That too. If I could get an extra long and wide piece of cloth, I could make a sling for him and be able to help out better."

"And your arms probably wouldn't get so tired." She sighs. "As soon as we finish this room, let's see if we can get you one."

That's motivation to finish the room quickly, though I still have only one free hand, and the other arm aches from the weight of constantly carrying Abby. She's still small, but not enough to make carrying her easy.

Together, we leave the room and head down the maze of hallways. It's like a never-ending battle with my memory, trying to keep track of everything in this place.

When we finally stop at a person, my chest fills with dread. It's the servant from this morning. Fredrick. How am I ever going to get what I need from someone so rude and callous?

"This tarnished has a request," the woman with me says.

Fredrick clucks in irritation and turns toward us. "Make it quick."

The tarnished nods at me. The last thing I want to do is plead my case to this man, but what other choice do I have? "I was wondering if I could get a large piece of cloth I could use to make a sling for the baby. I need to keep him with me at all times, but I can't be as efficient working with only one hand. If I could make a sling, I'd be able to better fulfill both my duties." And not have my arms killing me at the end of the day.

"How do I know you won't just use the cloth to make more clothes?"

"You can check up on me if you wish."

"The last thing I want to do is take time out of my day for a tarnished."

I clench my teeth at the harsh tone. I hope I was never this rude to any tarnished. "I can promise I will use the cloth for the purpose of carrying the baby."

"Promise of a tarnished is worth nothing." Fredrick clicks his tongue. "Fine. I was told to keep the baby happy and well taken care of, if anything came to me. This seems in the best interest of the baby. Go get your cloth."

A *thank you* pricks the tip of my tongue, but I can't bring myself to say it. Not to him, when he's so clearly trying to do what's best for himself, and not what's needed.

The other tarnished gives him a little nod and backs away. I go with her. Once we're out of earshot, she says, "You've been blessed to get something. Let's go grab it now and get you situated."

We go to the laundry room, where there are plenty of clean pieces of cloth to choose from. I pick one, wrap it around me, and place Abby inside to create a sort of protective pouch. She looks up at me, her little eyes twinkling. I only wish I had something real for her eyes to twinkle about.

"Thank you for your help," I tell the other tarnished.

"Of course. That baby of Chancellor Stephen's is a top priority." By the way she gazes at the baby, I know Abby's not just a priority, but loved and cherished. At least there's something small I can give her in this house of pain.

CHAPTER 6

The sling seems like a good idea at first, and it serves its purpose. The problem is Abby seems to enjoy it for now, but she needs to get out and about. Start moving and wiggling. Practice rolling. She'll never learn to crawl if she's always strapped to me. It's hard not to worry about her development.

She's a good baby, at least, rarely crying as long as I keep her clean and fed. Hiding her gender is easier than I thought it would be. No one likes changing a baby's diaper, even if everyone likes to fawn over her when we're not in the company of warlocks or untarnished women.

So far there's been no sign of Zade or Nathaniel. There are many places yet to explore, but not much of a chance to. I'm run ragged every day. Poor Abby is sweet, but the added weight on top of taking care of her doesn't help my exhausted state.

Father hasn't called for her yet, though I have helped clean his rooms several times when he isn't there. Nothing more than I used to do back home, only now his rooms are four times the size they once were, and I don't have my sisters working at my side.

Oh, how I miss them. I hope they survived and are now all in Envado. Knowing them, if they did, at the very least Serena,

Cynthia, and Waverly are trying to figure out a plan to rescue me. It's no use, though. We had more help than we could have ever dreamed at the last battle, only the tarnished weren't there, and we still couldn't win. How will they ever manage to do so now?

I find an empty room Abby can kick around in. The only thing is I have no clue if I'm allowed to use it or not. I think I can because it's for the baby and not me, but rules are so strict here.

I find the tarnished woman I've been working with and ask, "Can I use an empty room for Benjamin to play in? He needs time to be free of this sling so he can develop properly."

"I don't see why not, as long as it doesn't interfere with your chores."

I try not to groan. Less and less sleep seems to be my lot in life. "Of course."

"Do you have a room already in mind?"

"I found one I think may work."

"Why don't you show it to me, and we can make sure it's not used for anything else?"

"It's this way." I lead the way, wondering how many empty areas never get used in this place. When we reach the room, I open the door. "This is it."

"This should be fine. It hasn't been used in all the time I've been here."

"How long have you been here?" I hope I'm not asking something rude. It's hard to know what is and isn't all right to ask in the tarnished culture I've just barely become a part of.

"Thirty-four years. Long enough to see this place go through a lot of changes, and yet somehow it's all still the same. Tarnished doing what they should. The Grand Chancellor ruling the place. It will never be different."

Just hearing this makes me feel like crying. No one should have such a life. "You've known the Grand Chancellor that long?"

"Oh, yes. He's one of those things that haven't changed in the least. Same as always."

That's something strange to ponder on.

"While I have you," she says, "some clothes were brought in for Ben. Let's go get them."

I follow her down. The silence while making our way there reminds me of the times at father's house when we had to be quiet or risk his wrath. Even now I suppose it could be a possibility with him living here. I shiver at the thought.

When we reach the laundry room, there are a few tarnished working away. The tarnished woman leads me straight to a pile of blue clothes. There are plenty of them at the very least, even if they are all blue. I always liked blue more than pink anyway.

Abby is set with clothes. At least one of us is being taken care of.

* * *

COOK IS busy making dinner when I drop by the kitchen to get Abby's goat milk. He grins and coos at Abby.

"He's such a sweet-natured little thing," Cook says.

"He's a good baby." It's still strange to call Abby a *he*. I don't know if I'll ever get used to it.

Cook pulls the milk out, puts it in a newly acquired bottle, and hands it to me. "I wish the two of you got to spend more time in the kitchen."

"I feel like I'm always coming back here for another bottle."

"Babies do eat a lot, and you have a lot of extra work carrying him around," Cook says. "Why don't you have a bowl of mush while you're here?"

As gross as I thought mush was at first, it's the only thing there is to eat, so it's almost grown on me. At least it staves off hunger. "Are you sure it's all right? I don't want to get either of us in trouble."

"I'm certain of it." He dishes out a bowl and hands it to me. "You just sit and enjoy."

"Thank you." I make certain Abby's bottle is balanced appropriately so she can eat before digging into my mush. It's not much, but the extra food will be helpful as I continue on with my chores for the day. "Tell me a little about yourself."

For once Cook looks upset. "There's not much to tell, I'm afraid."

"What do you mean?" I hope I'm not upsetting him more. It's just that he's such a nice guy. I'd like to get to know him better.

"I've spent most of my life working here. Before I came here, I was at a home where young boys go after they've been tarnished."

I think of my experience being tarnished and can't imagine having that happen when one was a child. It's heart wrenching to think about. But the way he speaks of his home is wistful, almost like he misses it. "What was the tarnished home like, if you don't mind me asking?"

"I don't mind at all. Those were the happiest years of my life," he says. "There were some adult tarnished that watched over us boys. Some stayed regularly and others were rotated over a certain amount of time. I know now they left because they found households to work in, but my favorites never left. They stayed and took good care of us. We were allowed to run and play and have freedom, as long as we stayed within the bounds of the property we used.

"We helped with chores, but it was not like it is here. Chores were a fun time. A race, to see who could get them done the fastest, sometimes. Other times, we were just happy to help out. It was a peaceful place."

Unlike here. Even though we're ignored, there's much work to be done, and none of it is fun. Maybe if we got a break, to run and have some freedom, things would feel different, but of course that's never going to happen. "Thank you for sharing that with me."

"Of course. I only wish I had a lump or two of sugar for your mush."

I move to the sink to wash my now empty bowl. "That would be nice, but I don't mind. It's just good to have something in my stomach."

"Good. Now let me see little Ben before you go."

I finish washing my bowl and turn toward Cook so he can see the baby.

"Sleeping," he says. "What a good little baby."

"It's just too bad he doesn't sleep when I'm ready to," I say, a laugh hovering near the surface.

"Well, if you ever need a hand, you just let me know. I'm happy to help however I can."

"You've already done more than you know." I head to my chores with a lighter step. It's not every day I get to know something more about the tarnished world, even though I'm a part of it. I just wish there was a way to go to the world Cook described, instead of being stuck in the Grand Chancellor's house. Better yet, to go back to before I was captured and fix all of this mess.

Serena

CHAPTER 7

I enter Waverly's house and am in awe of its opulence. Not only is it large, but it's filled with spells sparkling everywhere. Spells dancing through the floor. Pictures made entirely of spells, the light moving around in a sort of abstract image. The temperature feels perfect in here— probably another spell.

"Serena." Molly tugs on my skirt and points to a particularly flashy spell. "What's that?"

I don't know the answer. Though I've been learning more about spells since I learned Cynthia could cast them, I still feel like a newborn babe when it comes to them. I'm much more comfortable with my gun and my wits. "I don't know, dearest."

Waverly returns from wherever she went down the hall and says, "We can move to the sitting room. The servants are making rooms for you as we speak."

As she guides us to the sitting room, I can't help but think of a nice bed. The only thing I want more than sleep is to have Bethany and Abigail back. I try not to think too hard about it as tears come to my eyes. I still can't fathom how we just left them there. We don't know where they ended up, only that they were caught by law officers. We almost all were. Only Cynthia's quick thinking and my gun saved us from her same fate.

Yet, what fate is it that's overcome Bethany and Abby? Will we ever find out? Wherever Abby is, I know Bethany will do her best to take care of her. I can't wait until the younger girls are out of the room. I must ask. "Any news on Bethany?"

Waverly's lips thin. "You're not going to like it."

"As if we'd like anything that happened." She at least has some news, which has me bouncing on my toes.

A servant walks in. Waverly says, "Would you please show these girls and Pernilla to their rooms?"

The girls and mother with little Benjamin wander out, while Cynthia and I stay behind.

A woman enters. "Let me introduce you to my mother," Waverly says.

"Pleased to meet you." I'm glad to know Zade's mother but want to move on to the information about Bethany. I expect she does as well as something might concern her son will come up. Hopefully it's something I'll be able to take some action against.

"And I you." She takes me by the hand. "Zade has told me so much about you."

The familiar choking feeling that comes whenever Zade is mentioned accosts me. "And he's told me much about you."

Cynthia blurts out, "What news do you have?"

Waverly grips the side of her chair. Her mother sits beside her to pour tea like a proper lady should. The familiar action puts me a little more at ease in a home full of nothing but differences.

"We've had word Bethany has been tarnished and is working in the Grand Chancellor's house," Waverly says.

I clutch my skirts, not believing it is really so. "You're certain?"

"Not positive, but fairly. It seems your father lives there, and Bethany is to work there, taking care of Abigail."

"And they just let her?" Cynthia asks.

"As far as we can tell. It's much harder to get information since the Grand Chancellor defeated us. We have less resources there."

My stomach churns at the memory of the fight, as if I'm riding in a carriage without a spell to help me. "Any word on Tawny?"

Waverly shakes her head while lowering her gaze. My heart sinks for her. At least I know where my sisters are; she has no news on one of her best friends. For all we know, Tawny could be long since dead, and there's nothing we can do about it.

"How can we help?" Cynthia asks.

Waverly shrugs. "We'll try to find out more, but until we do so, we're blind."

"We can't continue to be blind," I say. "I'll go back to Chardonia myself, if that's what it takes to get more information and get her and Abby out of there."

"I know you're worried," Waverly's mother says, "but we need to think this through carefully."

"But what else can we do?" I ask.

"Perhaps now they have dropped the spelling of tarnished tattoos and just limit the tarnished to certain areas instead, we can have Katherine go in and nose about," Waverly says.

"It'd be very dangerous for her," Cynthia replies.

"She'd have better access than most of Sanos still left in Chardonia," I say.

"I'll send a message to her right away," Waverly says. "I won't force her if she doesn't want to, but I have a feeling she will."

My heart settles a little more, for the moment. It will take time, but maybe we can get Bethany and Abby some help. I only hope it's not too late.

Bethany

CHAPTER 8

W e're to clean the Grand Chancellor's rooms today, something I've never done before. Just thinking of it gives me the chills. The last thing I want is to be closer to him or where he spends a lot of his time. I can't imagine what his rooms will be like—not like I want to. What he does in public, how he treats people, makes me sick. How much worse are his own personal rooms?

"You'll be by yourself, typically," the tarnished woman I first met says. "We take turns, each doing a part of his rooms because it's a big chore."

"Why not have a group of people working on them then?"

"In case the Grand Chancellor comes in. He doesn't like having us around in his private rooms."

We reach his rooms from the servants' entrance. It's a small door, located to the side of his bedroom. She peeks in, and after finding it clear, leads me inside. "If he comes while you're cleaning, you need to make your way here as quickly as possible and leave. Anyone he sees in here is never heard from again."

"How do you know he saw them if they're never heard from again?"

"Rumors. The Grand Chancellor probably tells people, though I don't know for sure. I'd just recommend getting out before you're seen."

"I can do that." It'll be like the worst sort of hex is after me. Being in his house is nerve-wracking enough.

I glance around the room, not surprised at how orderly it is. Everything has a place to the point of being creepy. Even though we haven't been through yet, his bed is perfectly made.

"Does he always make his own bed?" I ask.

"Every time I've come in, it's made."

How odd.

The rest of the room is just as neat. The few things in here are perfectly in place. Not a paper is out on the desk, nor a pen. There's no sofa or chair in the bedroom, though there's plenty of room for one of each. The room is mostly empty, devoid of life except for the few overly neat things he has left.

There's a giant collection of books with brown leather encasing them. They all look the same except each has a number printed on the bottom of the spine. As I move to dust the shelf, I notice there are fifty-four of them. I wonder what they could possibly be, so many of them and without titles, to boot.

As we clean, I can't help but feel like this isn't really the Grand Chancellor's room. More like no one's room. Except for the books, perhaps, there's no indication someone lives in it.

After we finish with the bedroom, we proceed to the bathroom, a dressing room, and a sitting room. They are as stale as the bedroom, with no hint of a life actually being led in these rooms.

"Is it always like this?" I ask the other tarnished I'm with.

"Always."

"Why do we need to spend so much time cleaning it, if it's already so clean?"

"Orders. Apparently, this is how the Grand Chancellor likes things."

I can't imagine anyone wanting things this way. "Would you keep your rooms like this, if you had one?"

"If I had one?" She stops cleaning, her eyes taking on a faraway look. "If I had one, it would be a warm place. Something full of love and happiness. A fire, for certain. Perhaps even cookies, despite being a bedroom."

"That's a lovely thought."

"Yes, well"—she gets back to cleaning more vigorously than before—"that's not the type of life I'll ever lead."

"Nor I, it would seem." Not when I have a few short months left to live.

CHAPTER 9

I creep into the Grand Chancellor's wife's room. It's tiny in comparison to the warlock's but still larger than the one I had at home. For the first time ever, I'm cleaning alone, though I'm not completely by myself as his wife is still in bed. I start with dusting the baseboards, a job I rarely did at home. They really take their cleaning seriously here.

Abby stirs. I stand and bounce her, trying to keep her quiet while I dust the furniture.

"Oh, it's one of you," the wife says. "I thought I heard a baby."

I turn so she can see Abby strapped to my front. Not speaking, especially to another female, is an odd thing to get used to.

She is worn and stretched, lines on her face making her look older than I suspect she is. Her hair is unkept and brown, and her eyes are a drab brown. What has she been through, living with the Grand Chancellor? How has he treated her? What evil has he cast upon her?

"It is a baby. A baby boy." Her previously lifeless voice perks up.

She pulls herself off the bed, and I see the elegant dressing gown is worn and ripped in places. The mistress of the house is as much a prisoner as I am. She may have more clothes than me, but mine are in better condition. She's small and tattered.

"Can I hold him?"

Though I feel bad for her situation, I don't want to let go of Abby. She's my responsibility. Plus, I don't want to risk the woman somehow finding out Abby is a girl. The more time other people spend holding her, the more likely it is to happen. But it's not like I can say no. I can't say anything at all. At least I'll be in the same room with them.

I unwrap Abby and hand her to the lady of the house. She snatches my sister up with a fervor that has me tense all over. Despite her eagerness, she sways the baby in her arms, gentler than I expect. Poor woman is just deprived of any attention.

"You can finish your chores," she says.

I realize I've been standing here, staring at them both and not doing a thing. The sooner I finish, the sooner I can hopefully have Abby back. As I get back to dusting, a terrible thought hits me. What if I can't have her back?

I steal a glance at the lady of the house. She gazes on Abby with undisguised longing. I move faster and finish the dusting in record time. Only problem is there are a lot more chores to be dealt with before I have an excuse to take my sister back and leave.

The chores seem to fade into the background as I do them, my whole focus being on the two of them. The woman is tender and loving. Even starts to hum a lullaby. It only makes me more nervous. What if she never gives Abby back? What will I do? What will happen when she discovers Abby is a girl?

My heart pounds a frantic rhythm as I take the sheets off the bed and put new ones on. There has to be something more I can do than sit here and clean while my sister is ripped away from me. I silently plead the woman will give back my sister.

When I finally finish, I go to her, remaining silent like I'm supposed to. On the inside, I'm screaming.

"I had a baby boy once. Nathaniel. I miss him."

Nathaniel. I clench my teeth to keep from saying anything, but I'm dying to ask her to say more. Where is he now? What happened to him? Why haven't I seen him yet?

"Babies are such treasures," she says.

I clench my fists within the folds of my skirt. I need my sister back. Now.

As if she's read my mind, she finally hands the baby back to me. I quickly wrap her up in my makeshift sling, unwilling to leave her within the woman's grasp any longer than I have to.

"Come often with the baby," she says.

As if I have a choice. I do what's ordered of me and hate every minute of it. There has to be something else I can do. Some way to get around all the stringent rules placed here.

She puts her hand on Abby's cheek. I want to step back, to move away from her—from being closer to another person than I have been since I arrived—but something about the longing in her gaze stops me.

"I never had another son. I should have." She speaks as if to herself. "Now he's getting a second, younger wife, while I waste away up here."

She pulls back, gives a large, humming sigh, and totters back to bed. I help her get comfortable under the sheets, tension leaving me now that my sister is safe. Having to live with the Grand Chancellor all these years, like his wife has, I don't know how she's managed to survive. Being tarnished is a much better fate than the one she's been dealt.

"Have Nathaniel sent to me, would you? I miss his quiet talks."

The urge to speak is almost overwhelming. Now I have an excuse to ask about his whereabouts. I only hope I like the answer I get.

CHAPTER 10

This not having a name thing is beyond ridiculous. I'm trying to find the woman who's been helping me since I arrived. She seems to be in charge—well, in charge below Fredrick, and there's no chance I'm asking him for help—but without a name, no one knows who I'm talking about. Usually she's easy to find, always around somewhere, yet now cleaning on my own, it's like she's become a ghost. I suppose we all are.

"What did her markings look like?" a male tarnished asks.

I try to bring up her tattoos in my mind's eye, but nothing comes. "I don't know."

"Keep track, because it's the only way to identify someone around here." He hurries back to his task without a second glance at me.

That is a good use of the tattoos, I suppose. I never really thought about it before. I touch my cheek as I head to the sleeping room. I don't know what mine look like. The few times I've been in a room with a mirror, I've avoided looking in it. I don't know how to reconcile who I am with what my outward appearance has become.

I peek in the sleeping room, the empty beds calling to me with an ache. I need the rest, but I want to ask about Nathaniel. I suppose I can ask anyone, but she's the one I know the best. The one I trust.

I brush my gaze across those sleeping, only to still not find her. I should just give up now and search for her tomorrow. With a sigh, I take Abby to the nearby empty room we use for her floor time. Laws knows she doesn't get enough of it.

Usually the room is empty of both people and furniture. Just a big open space with big windows. Only this time, it's not empty. The woman I've been seeking is here, looking out one of those big windows. She doesn't turn as I enter but stays staring out at the expanse of gray clouds.

I take Abby out of her sling and quickly change her nappy, ready to hide her gender should the woman turn around. She never does. Once Abby's changed, I let her stretch and kick while I coo.

This finally gets the woman's attention. She comes over nearby, a smile trying to turn her lips up as she watches us but having a difficult time of it. No one should have such sorrow carried through their life that they can't even smile.

"Do you ever get tired of this?" The sound of my voice startles me. I don't get to hear it often any more.

The woman points to the walls and then cups her hands around her ears. While she nods her head, she says, "It's the life we're given. I'm content with it."

Someone is listening. Or could be, I suppose. It's hard to know anything for certain in this house.

"He's such a cute baby," she says, coming over to sit on the floor by us. "The Chancellor must be very pleased with him."

I don't bother to tell her the Chancellor is my father and hasn't once sent to see his son. Sure, he's pleased, but not enough to be bothered by it all. Works out best for us, and I'm counting on it staying this way. I don't want to have to be around my father more.

What I want to ask her now is how someone is listening all the time. Who is it exactly, and how are they doing it? I assume a spell is involved, but I can't imagine the Grand Chancellor sitting around, listening to us. Maybe it's one of his law officers, or a warlock who has to work for him to pay off a debt but has just enough magic to listen in on conversations. Possibly both or some combination I haven't thought of.

"I had a request from the mistress of the house," I say.

"Oh?" The woman barely pays me heed as she tickles Abby's cheeks.

Here it goes. Please let me get some information from this. If he's dead, I have to know it. "She was wondering if she could see her son, Nathaniel."

"That's not possible."

My heart sinks to the floor. He's gone, then. That's it. His sticking up for us, trying to help, brought his father's wrath so harshly he's no longer on this world. I feel like I should say something, but I don't know what. I suppose I wasn't as familiar with him like I am with my sisters, so I don't know how much of a right I have to mourn him, but I do anyway.

The time we spent together, he talked to me like I mattered. Like my thoughts and opinions meant something. His meant something to me, in return. He was quickly becoming my best friend, even though we didn't get to speak nearly as much as I would have liked.

"He's growing fast," the woman says, knocking me from my thoughts.

I nod, already growing used to not speaking when spoken to. She continues to play with the baby until she has to go to work and I have to go to sleep. As I get both Abby and myself ready for bed, my thoughts linger on Nathaniel. It wasn't much, really, just a few conversations here and there. But it felt like more. Almost like I want to reach out and touch him. It felt like something that should never end, and now he's even more out of my reach than he was before.

CHAPTER 11

L ater this week, I'm scrubbing the floor, pushing all my
might into the job. It's the only way I know to ease the pain
of everything that's happened. Abby seems to enjoy the process
and quickly falls asleep with my movements.

She's a spoiled little thing, despite the harsh life I have. This
constant having her by me and rocking her makes it difficult to
get her to sleep at night. She fusses when I try to lie down. She
wants to be continually rocked. Unfortunately, I can't do that
when I'm trying to get rest.

My body aches from all the chores and the extra weight. My
eyes drift close, only to open again. I can't fall asleep on the job. I
don't know what they'd do to me, but I can't imagine it'd be good.
We're supposed to be invisible, not asleep where people walk by.
The main hall is definitely a place where people walk by.

Once I'm finished, I pour the bucket of dirty water outside and
head to the laundry room to help scrub dirty clothes. It's a nasty
job—one that makes me wish scrubbing the floor had taken
longer. Clothing is one of the few things in this house that actually gets a chance to grow dirty.

There's only one other tarnished present as I enter the laundry room. A tall one. If I didn't know better, I'd say she's an Envadi and not a tarnished. But that can't be. She's bald, just like me, and has lines swirled across her face. She scrubs the clothes madly, like they have done her some wrong. Maybe they have.

She looks familiar. All morning, I keep trying to look at her without making it appear like I'm looking at her. It's ridiculous, really. I don't want her to feel self-conscious about me staring at her, especially when people tend to overlook us more than anything else, but I can't help but think I know her from somewhere.

My hands grow red from the hot water, and my fingers are raw. The stains on some of these clothes I don't dare guess what they're from. This is a gross job. The other girl keeps the same ferocious tendency on cleaning the clothes. Maybe she is just that hard of a worker.

But it seems like something else to me. It niggles at the back of my mind. Who is she? Why does she seem like someone I should know?

Finally, I can't stand it any longer. "I'm sorry. You look so familiar. Have we met before? Have you been a tarnished in another household?"

"It's not likely we've met. Before this house, I was not a tarnished. I just became one a short while ago." Even her accent sounds like an Envadi.

"Me too."

"Were you captured after the fight?" she asks.

This is dangerous to be speaking of. I nod.

"Me too."

I glance around the room. When no one is in sight, I chance sending a note spell, knowing it could get me sacrificed. Besides, I'm to be sacrificed anyway, and I think for once, it's worth it. If she is who I think she is, she has as much reason to do magic as I do. Instead of having the spell note fly off to the recipient, I let it hover here. 'My name is Bethany.'

She widens her eyes as she takes me in. She drops the sheet she was holding and hurries to spell back, 'I'm Tawny.'

Tawny. She's not dead, just captured. I wish there was a way to get the news to Waverly. She has to be dying to know. Tawny's family has to be dying to know. At least, I assume she has a family. I don't know that much about her, other than she helped me learn a lot of spells, back when we were living in the caves. She's very talented.

'I can't believe you're alive,' I spell to her, trying to make out her features beneath all her tattoos.

'I can't believe we're both tarnished.'

'That either.'

'Do you have any way to contact the outside world?'

I shake my head.

'Drat,' she spells. 'I have to let my family know I'm alive and where I am.'

'I wish there was a way I could help.'

'This is a place without hope.'

The statement echoes within me, resonating more than I like.

CHAPTER 12

Now I know Tawny's here, I try to see her as often as I can. We both have a hard time being around each other, though. It's like a memory from the past we can't quite grasp on to.

She eats breakfast while I feed Abby. The cook has been more than true to his word, letting me get milk whenever I need it.

"I just can't wait until he's old enough that I can give him treats," he says.

I laugh, though the sound is mellowed by the circumstances. It's nice to have her fawned over.

The tarnished woman I first met while here—who I've now come to think of as Three, for she has three lines across her nose—comes and gets me as soon as breakfast is over, which of course never takes long. She sets a brisk pace for the hall that leads to the door outside, the one through which we all go to the outhouse.

"Where are we headed this morning?" I hope it's not to clean the outhouse. That's one job I definitely don't want.

"You're to work outside today," she says. "We're all to gain as many skills as possible, so we can do whatever job is needed."

"I haven't much experience with working outside."

"You'll learn."

"Will you be teaching me?"

"Not today, I'm afraid. I work outside on occasion, to keep my skills fresh, but I mostly am in charge of everything running smoothly on the inside."

That she does, with great skill. We walk out of the house, the crisp air refreshing against my skin. It should be cool like this for a while yet, before it starts to warm, but there's still plenty of work to be done, from the looks of all the tarnished we pass.

"How many tarnished are there in this place?" I ask.

"Over fifty. It's a lot of people to take care of."

"A lot of shadows to hide in," I mutter. I never would have guessed there are so many of us. Though I suppose, with how big the house is combined with how clean the Grand Chancellor likes to keep it, fifty may not actually be enough.

We continue walking through the grounds. They're lavish, but now I think about it, they're almost too orderly. Bushes and shrubs cut back. Flowers in perfect patterns. Bright yellows, blues, pinks, and purples. The air is scented with sweet floral aroma, but not a sound can be heard. Not a weed in sight. More to show something is wrong with the Grand Chancellor.

When we get to a tarnished, a man with lots of muscles and dirt, we finally stop. This place is huge. Having spells covering this entire area proves how powerful the Grand Chancellor is.

"This is your helper for the day. She just needs to be shown a little bit about working outside, in case she's ever needed out here," Three says.

"Today's a good day for it. We've got a lot of tasks ahead."

Inwardly, I groan. I was hoping at the very least there would be a break from how hard things are, but it doesn't sound like it.

"Is the baby warm enough?" Three asks.

"He's snug in his sling, with a blanket," I reply.

"Good. If it gets too cold out here for him, you are allowed to run in and get more blankets before continuing on with your chores."

And I bet I still have the same number of chores. "Thank you. I'll make certain he's well taken care of."

This seems to satisfy her, as she gives me an almost smile before heading back into the house.

"Well," the gardener says, "best get on with our work for the day. Take that wheel barrow and follow me."

He grabs a wheel barrow of his own while I snatch the one he pointed to, which is full of leaves, and we walk through the expansive grounds. Again. I thought going back and forth through the big house all day was a chore in and of itself, but the grounds are worse. At least there are no stairs here. Though there are some hills, we aren't going near them today.

We come to an area spelled in full with a pale-yellow light and surrounded by a brick wall. As we enter in a wrought-iron gate that's been left open, the gardener says, "These are the vegetable gardens. They're spelled to stay the perfect temperature year round."

And it's true. The moment I walk in the gate through the spell, it's like a warm sunny day. If we stay in here very long, I'll be sweaty, and Abby will need blankets taken off of her. The area is huge, covering a vast amount of land in various stages of growth.

Pumpkins several times bigger than Abby are in one row. The next, peas, plump and ready to be picked. Carrot tops feather across another line. More and more vegetables farther than I can see.

"Over here"—he points to tall stalks of corn and many other green things—"are plants about ready to be harvested. Next to them we have plants that will be harvested in the next few weeks. As you continue to head down the path, the plants are in lower and lower stages of development. We're at the very end today."

I follow him down the path, and indeed, the farther we go, the less developed the vegetation is. When we get to the end, there's a wide area with no plants at all and a few piles of leaves on the dirt.

"This is where we'll be bringing everything today." He dumps leaves out of his wheelbarrow onto an empty spot and motions for me to do the same. Once I maneuver the wheelbarrow where it belongs and dump it out, I'm already sweating.

"Any questions so far?" he asks.

"None that I can think of."

"Then get to work. Go back where you met me, use the rake and shovel to gather leaves, and bring them back here. If you have any questions, I'll be in here, weeding."

At least I don't have to stay in here. I've picked more needed plants than weeds, the few times I've tried. Besides, I kind of like the briskness to the air outside. Or outside of this spell. One like this would have been helpful when we were in our cave, to generate food for all those people. I'll have to keep it in mind for the future. A future I don't have. Never mind.

As I walk back toward the leaves, I think about my future and how I don't really have much of one. I wish I knew how much time was left until the tournament. It doesn't make a difference, though. No matter how long the time, I'm still to be sacrificed, and right now I can't see a way out of it

There are no clocks in the house. No calendars to show the passage of time. No way to know when I'm to be sacrificed. I thought it would help, not knowing. Instead it's maddening. Time moves so slowly, yet it moves quickly toward my eventual death.

I stop as I get to the leaf pile and realize how close I am to the road. So close, it wouldn't take long to reach it at all. The only thing that stands between me and it is a faint gray spell, domed over the entire area of the Grand Chancellor's property. It must be the death spell, if I leave. Or maybe it's the one that stop spells from getting out. Either way, it's a formidable barrier.

As I rake the leaves into a pile, I can't help peeking at the road and how tantalizingly close it is. Too close for me to just ignore.

What if they tell everyone the spell is there to kill you if you try to escape, but in reality, it's just the spell to keep magic inside the property? Or maybe it's not even that. Maybe the Grand Chancellor just likes a gray pall cast over his world. It would fit his personality.

I realize I've stopped raking. I take a step forward. I could try it, just a little bit. There's nothing here to stop me. I'm going to die at the tournament anyway. Why not die trying to escape this place?

I take another step forward and another, until I'm next to the gray spell. All I have to do is reach my hand out, and I'll cross the spell. That's all it'll take to see if it works. I can do this.

Abby stirs. I can't do this. I can't leave her. If nothing else, she needs me. If I die, what will happen to her? Nothing good—of that I can be certain. I step away from the spell to get back to my wheelbarrow.

"Good choice," the gardener says, startling me. "I've seen more than one tarnished killed that way."

Guess I made the right choice then. If he's telling the truth. I think I believe him, which means I really am stuck here.

CHAPTER 13

I'm working in the laundry room until my hands are raw when Fredrick enters. I scrub harder. I'm not sure whether it's from wanting to appear like I'm working to his satisfaction or because my frustration at having to deal with a man so filled with his power, when he really has none, needs an outlet.

Next to me, Tawny is scouring just as hard. The two of us have been silent all morning, and his arrival makes me grateful we were. We could have been caught spelling messages to each other. The thought makes me scrub even harder. My muscles are going to pay for this later, but I can't bring myself to care at the moment.

"What have we in here?" Fredrick moves to the linens hanging on the far side of the room to dry. He grabs a sheet with two fingers, like it will somehow contaminate him. "This is filthy. You haven't cleaned it nearly well enough."

I clench my jaw, as he rips it from the line and throws it in my pile. He does so with another and another, declaring each time how dirty they are.

They are cleaner than he is.

"Get these cleaned up and do a better job on them. The Grand

Chancellor doesn't stand for a mess in his house." With that, he storms out the door.

I want to yell after him. To call him the names he is and demand he clean the sheets if he thinks they are so bad. But I'm not in a position to do anything.

Nothing at all.

CHAPTER 14

E arly the next morning, I'm getting ready to head to my usual chores when Three stops me.

"I have a new job to add to your duties today," she says. "The last tarnished on the job has fallen ill."

Just what I need. Another duty to add to my day. "What job is that?"

"You're to clean the Grand Chancellor's son's room and bring him his meals."

"Why would Nathaniel need to eat?" I ask, the statement not fully making it through my thought process.

"The same reason the rest of us need to."

Shock courses through me. "Do you mean he's alive?" My words come out loud and bold.

She looks at me, startled. "What? You thought he was dead?"

"Well, yes. The big fight. And then he's never been around."

"Ah, that explains it," she replies. "The Grand Chancellor was furious with him. Didn't want him killed, though. He's locked in his room as punishment. You're to help look after his needs now. We, tarnished, and the Grand Chancellor are the only ones allowed in. Anyone else is stopped by a spell if they try."

"Oh." For the first time, I'm not just glad I'm a tarnished, I'm downright grateful. Finally it will be of some use, other than just making me able to be in a room while someone is talking without them noticing me.

"You're to tend him," she says. "He needs three meals a day and his room cleaned twice, once in the morning and once at night. New sheets brought in every morning. You need to do all that on top of your other chores."

I try to look as upset as possible because I know that's how I'm supposed to feel right now, but all I feel is joy. Not only is he alive, but I get to see him. Bring him food and clean his room. Well, cleaning his room I could do without, but it means I'll have a chance to see him. Not to talk. If the walls really do have ears, his room is sure to have the most of them.

"You start right now. His breakfast tray should be ready. Take it up with your cleaning supplies."

If I wasn't so excited about this all, I'd be very put out over not only having to carry Abby and his breakfast, but also all the cleaning supplies.

I grab the tray with one hand and move to my cleaning supplies with the other. I balance the tray as I shove the few items not in my bucket inside, grateful there's running water in this house. I pick up the bucket, making certain nothing spills on the breakfast tray.

All I can think on the way to where I was instructed is to not sneeze. Or trip. Or anything else that'd make me spill. I don't want to do anything that will either make me take longer to get to him or ruin my chances of serving him. There won't be any other way to see him if I don't.

I'm grateful for the weeks I've spent doing chores that have strengthen my muscles, allowing me to do this task, though it's still difficult. When I come to his door, I set my bucket down and take the breakfast tray with both hands. I take a deep breath, wondering what exactly I'm going to find behind this door.

Will he care to see me? Will he be the same person I remember, or will his imprisonment have changed him? What's more, will he even recognize me? Will he know who I am, now that I'm bald and covered in tattoos? Does it matter if he does?

I wish I had more time. More time to sort out all these thoughts in my head. More time to accept he's alive.

Before I can work up the courage to knock on the door, there's a thud from the room. What was that? I pound on the door, hoping it's not the Grand Chancellor hexing Nathaniel. If he is, I swear I will fight him until my last bit of magic is gone.

The door bursts open, and I balance the breakfast tray in one hand, ready to throw it as a distraction, while I stretch the other out, ready to cast a spell. Only as soon as my hand crosses the door line, Nathaniel takes a hold of it.

Neither of us says anything, despite there being so much that needs to be said. When you live in a house where everything is heard, you can't say even the most trivial of things without consequences.

But the way his hand wraps around mine, it feels like we should have held hands the first time we met and never let go.

Even with a job to do, I don't want to let go. I hand him the food tray, which he balances with his free hand, and grab my bucket. I go inside, kick the door shut behind me, and put the bucket on the ground while he puts the food tray down on a small table.

Then he wraps his arms around me, which is perfect, except for the baby napping between us. I want to laugh, but don't dare to, so instead I grin up at him, while he beams down at me. It feels as if I could stay like this forever.

Unfortunately, I can't.

When he finally pulls back, we look at each other. Nathaniel. Alive and well, standing before me more perfect than ever. Except he is looking a little pale, and his eyes are wide, though he's grown more muscular since I last saw him, something I wouldn't have expected with him locked up all the time. He grips his hands together like his life depends on it.

I realize I've been staring at him for far too long. And I'm still staring. I force myself to drag my gaze away from him. I bend down to grab my cleaning supplies. It takes every ounce of will power I have not to turn toward him. Not to talk to him. To do anything but carry on with my duties like I'm supposed to.

I'm not the person I used to be. I'm not the girl who enjoyed the times we had together. I'm grateful he's alive, but that's where it needs to end. He probably was so excited to see me because I'm another person, something he rarely sees anymore except whoever usually cleans his room. There's no way he recognized me. Not with how I look now. And with those wide eyes, he looks frightened of me. Like I'm not supposed to collide with this part of his life.

I suppose I'm not. If I was, I would have seen him before now. I've been here long enough. It should have happened. Maybe he'll ask for another tarnished to bring his food and clean his room. That'll be good. Then he won't have to see what I've become. That's what I tell myself as I walk toward the window to begin cleaning it.

But each step is harder to take. And each step knows I'm getting farther from the one thing I want and never thought I would see again.

I get to the window and set down my cleaning supplies. I reach down toward the bucket when I realize I don't have any water. This is perfect. The last thing I want is to make that walk again. Instead of doing so, I grab a rag to dust the baseboards.

"Wait," he says.

My breathing is rigid. I can't turn around. Can't move forward. Can't do anything. It's because I'm following his command; that's all. He's one of my owners now. I'm just doing what he ordered. But why isn't he saying anything else? Why am I just standing here, looking out the window, not seeing anything?

If he wanted something, shouldn't he be giving me another order? I want to know—I'm dying to know—but I can't bring myself to turn around. Even without seeing him, I can feel his presence. This strong magnifying thing that pulls at me, drawing me to him. Except I'm still frozen in place.

It's as if some invisible weight is holding me there, keeping me where I can hear the sound of his voice but don't have to show my face to him. I can't even turn to see him. Maybe it's a spell. I'm facing away from him, so maybe I just missed the flash of color that zipped toward me and froze me in place.

My body keeps running hot and cold, like I'm sick. What is wrong with me?

Suddenly, there are hands on my shoulders. I'm turned around, wrapped back in his arms, and wrapping my arms around him. I've dreamed of holding him like this for so long, but we never, ever touched. Yet here I am in his room, and we're wrapped in each other. He's saying something, but I can't understand the words. Can't understand anything except the warm, protective feel of him pressing me tight against him.

And then I break.

For so long, I've been holding everything all in, staying strong, especially for Abby, but now it doesn't matter. Tears come raging out, fast and hard, but thankfully silent. He must know I'm crying anyway, because he rubs his hand on my back and continues to hold me. And... did he just kiss the top of my head? My tears slow, as I wonder if I really felt what I thought I did.

As sweet as this is, Abby is trapped between us and starting to wiggle. We pull apart.

He casts a spell. I flinch, but it's just words floating through the air. We never seem to get in trouble for casting spells, so I assume the Grand Chancellor doesn't have something watching all the spells in the house.

His spell says, 'I can't believe it's you. What happened, Bethany?'

I read the words three times, before I can think again. He knows it's me. Despite all the changes that have happened to me, he hasn't hesitated at all to know it's me. Yet, I'm hesitating. Even though he knows I can do magic, it's hard to do any in front of another person when I've been working so hard at not letting my powers be known. But this is Nathaniel. I can trust him.

I cast my own spell, overriding my fear to spell out, 'I was captured trying to help my family escape to Envado. Now I'm tarnished and set to be sacrificed at the tournament.'

He scrunches up his face like he's in pain as he gives my hand a quick squeeze and glances over my neck. He spells out, 'Oh, Bethany. I'm so sorry. This is all my fault."

I give an unhappy laugh before replying, 'Your fault? How in the world is it your fault?'

'If I had been strong enough to defeat my father, you wouldn't have had to go through this.'

'You did your best.' Though I wish he had been strong enough. I wish we'd all been strong enough. Even with everyone trying to defeat the Grand Chancellor at the same time, it wasn't enough. There's no way to beat that warlock.

'But he made me take all that magic from those five girls when I had to fight Cynthia in the tournament,' he spells back. 'It should have been enough.'

'How much has he taken over the years?'

He sighs and sits back on a chair. 'Too many.'

This we can both agree on, even if we'll never know the exact number. While he thinks everything over, I work on dusting off the base boards. I've only cleaned a little spot when he's right there next to me, dusting right along with me.

I spell out, 'You don't have to help.'

'I want to.'

A warm, peaceful feeling settles in my chest. Together we work in silence, first dusting off the boards, and then he helps me wash the windows and the bathroom and sweep the floor. We're able to finish much faster than if I worked alone.

As I gather my cleaning supplies, he spells, 'Why don't you help me eat breakfast?'

'I shouldn't.' My stomach growls at the thought of food, betraying me.

'Please. It's lonely being locked up all the time, and I've missed talking with you.'

It's the please that does me in, not that we can actually do any talking. He pulls a second chair close to his table and has me sit down before taking a seat himself. We don't send many spells to each other while we eat. Just enjoy being with the company. Toward the end of the meal, Abby gets fussy. I stand and bounce to calm her down.

'Who is the little boy?' Nathaniel spells to me.

Part of me wants to tell him the truth about her being my sister, but even though I trust him fully, I can't risk anyone else knowing. Especially not if he talks with his father. I doubt he would say anything, but the Grand Chancellor has ways of persuading things out of people. The Grand Chancellor has ways of doing a lot of things.

'My little brother,' I reply with a spell. 'Father wanted me to care for him until he's old enough to learn and get a tutor.' Unless I'm dead before then, of course. In all likelihood, I will be.

'And you have to clean, still?'

'Yes, but it's a good thing. Otherwise I wouldn't have found you.'

'I'm glad you did.'

'Me too.'

It feels strange that we've spent all this time together yet haven't said a word. I prefer talking over doing spells. If I keep this up for long, I will be weak within the hour. Then where will I be if I need my magic? Of course, everyone I'd go up against would be so much stronger than me, not because I'm weak, but because the Grand Chancellor keeps the strongest of warlocks around all the time. Even if I had my magic intact, it wouldn't matter.

'I should be going.' Plenty more work to do before the day is over and I struggle to get some sleep.

'I hope you can come back again.'

'They said this was part of my new duties, so I'm certain I will.'

'Good. The time won't go nearly fast enough.'

'For me either,' I spell out.

It's hard to stand. Even harder to walk toward the door. Before I leave, I glance back to find him watching me. I give a little wave, and he waves back.

'I hope to see you soon,' he spells to me with vivid red floating letters.

I wish I could take the spelled note with me, to have something to remember this day by. I'll just have to trust that it happened, and that I'll be back again.

CHAPTER 15

I return at lunch and again at dinner with trays of food and then cleaning supplies with the latter. Though we scrubbed his room clean just this morning, orders say we do it again. He offers to help, but this time I shoo him away to eat while I give the room a quick once over.

As soon as I'm done, we continue catching up. We spell out notes about all that's happened between when he was captured and when I met him in his room.

'My father has been coming to see me once a week since he locked me up.'

I glance at the door, worried the Grand Chancellor will suddenly appear.

'Don't worry. He only comes on Sunday evenings.'

'What day even is it? It's so easy to lose track.'

'It is for me, too. I only know because of my Sunday visits, and even then it's hard to keep track of. Today is Tuesday.'

It's strange to think of something as normal as what day of the week it is. 'Does he stay to visit very long?'

'Depends on how much he feels like scolding me.'

I put my hand on his, and warmth trickles through me. 'I'm sorry you have to go through that.'

'Don't be. What you're going through is so much worse.'

I sigh, thinking how tough we both have it. At least I get to move about a larger area, even if I'm still in a prison. Prison.

'Where are the dungeons?'

He narrows his eyes. 'Why do you want to know?'

'Zade.'

'I should have guessed.'

'I just want to pass him a note. Let him know what's happened.'

'It's too dangerous to even attempt.'

I can't imagine what exactly Zade's going through right now, but I can imagine the words that would lift him up. I wish Nathaniel would allow me to know, even if I never used the information. He's probably right, though. If I knew, I'd almost assuredly try and find a way to visit, and the last thing I need right now is to get in trouble. I don't want to risk losing my visits with Nathaniel or losing care over Abby. If anyone else is in charge of her, I'm certain her gender won't stay secret for long.

'I know it is,' I spell out, my words glowing green and tinted with grey frustration, 'but it's hard to be in the same building as him and not be able to do anything about it.'

'I understand completely. I used to take him and some of the other prisoners extra food when I could manage it. Now, I can't even do that.'

'Are there many prisoners?'

'More than there should be.'

'Why are they all there?'

'I don't know about most of them. It seems some are there for the same reasons as Zade—they've done something to cross my father.'

'Your father isn't someone I want to cross.'

'And yet here you are, crossing him just by talking with me. Every spell you cast is a way to defy him.'

'I never thought of it like that.' And though I am ultimately to be sacrificed, it's gratifying to know there is something I can do to oppose his rules.

Cynthia

CHAPTER 16

"Cynthia, wait up," Serena calls out to me. She and Waverly hurry to meet me in the gardens.

As I wait for them, I enjoy the beauty. Or try to enjoy it. It's difficult with so much weighing on the mind. The garden is spelled to be the perfect temperature. Despite the coolness outside, it's balmy inside the grounds. It smells like the right amount of floral scent while birds sing their sweet tune.

Cobblestone pathways twist around the grounds. The flowers are thriving, many of them with bright colors you don't find in nature, or a certain sparkle that would never be, glittering in the sunlight. Spells abound in this country. I've learned so many new ones, but it doesn't help my heart. It's heavy with the loss of my sisters. Heavy with the weight of knowing I didn't save them from whatever fate has befallen them.

"We have news from Katherine," Waverly says as soon as they reach me.

My heart lifts, though it's ready to tremble with fear. News doesn't mean good things. At least we won't be so lost in the unknown. It's what I tell myself as I gear up for news that could be the worst I've encountered. "What is it?"

"She was able to get news through a driver who delivers goods there. Apparently, Bethany is at the Grand Chancellor's. Things get a little weird after that. The driver said Benjamin was there with her."

"But he's here with us," Serena says.

"She must have figured a way to hide Abby's gender. That would explain why they're still together. Otherwise, who knows what would have happened to the baby?" Waverly says.

"Any news on how Bethany is holding up?" I hope she's managing. She always had such a quiet spirit about her. I don't know if she'll be able to maintain it, or if the Grand Chancellor's house will break her.

"Very little. The Grand Chancellor works them hard."

I clench my teeth. I hate to think of sweet Bethany having to go through that.

"There is more," Waverly says. "The Grand Chancellor is marrying again, taking a second wife."

My chest tightens at the wrongness of that thought. "Bless the poor girl that becomes his wife."

"She'll have a hard journey in front of her. That's certain," Serena says.

"What's more, the Queen of Envado is getting anxious about her daughter, and the entire situation going on with Chardonia," Waverly says. "I don't know if we can keep her from storming in there much longer."

"But Tawny could be..." Dead. I let my words trail off, not trusting myself to speak.

"I know."

And if the Queen storms in there without knowing more, there will be heavy losses on both sides. Especially after the last war we tried to win. The Grand Chancellor is exceptionally strong. If Envado joins this war, they may have losses more serious than they expect. "We need a plan. A good plan."

"Do you have something in mind?"

I think a minute, hoping the idea developing will work. If it won't, not only will we have no news for the Queen, but lives will be on the line. "We need someone to break into the Grand Chancellor's house after the wedding. To join the party."

"Rather risky, isn't it?" Serena says.

"Yes, but if we can get a note to Bethany, to open up communications, it will all be worth it."

"I think you're right," Waverly says. "I know a man who might be able to do it."

"Tell me all about him. I want to deliver the idea in person."

"You can't go back to Chardonia," Serena says.

"I need to. Not only do Bethany and Abby need me, but I can't continue to sit around here, doing nothing. It's driving me mad."

"What will Lukas say?"

"That I'm crazy, but he'll understand I have to go. He'll probably even come with me."

Serena bites her lip. "You have to promise me you'll stay safe. You can't go taking more risks than you absolutely have to."

"I promise to try my best. I'll send back as much information as I can." It's the only thing I can give her. For the first time since we entered Envado, I feel as if there's finally something I can do to help.

Bethany

CHAPTER 17

As I wash windows, my thoughts travel to the time when I first met Nathaniel. It ended up being one of the best things that happened in my life. I'm forever grateful for that day, when I was at the tournament Cynthia was participated in.

He and I bumped into each other. Literally. He was going one way, and I was going another way looking back at something. I don't even remember what it was now. And then we collided.

I gasped, afraid he would hex me for certain. My heart pounded against my ribcage, like it wanted to beat through my chest. I drew in on myself.

But he just looked at me. And looked. And looked.

"I'm sorry," I mumbled.

"Don't worry about it. It was as much my fault as it was yours," he said.

My head felt faint, like I'd pass out from shock. Warlocks never claimed such things. Not ever.

The look on my face must have been something else because the next thing I knew, he was laughing.

I worked up the courage to ask, "What's so funny?"

"The look on your face." Just as I suspected. He continued. "I've never seen a look like that before. Sorry for laughing. I just can't help it."

My feet seemed to melt into the ground. I couldn't move. Not an inch. I was too fascinated by him.

"You can say something," he said. "It's all right."

"I… I wasn't looking where I was going." I kept my head lowered.

"Neither was I. Truth is, I'm kind of in a hurry." He looked over my shoulder. "In fact, I should be going. Sorry again for running into you."

He hurried off. I turned to watch him go, feeling different than I'd ever felt before.

I kept thinking about him until I found him the next day on accident, while I was out with a tarnished.

"Hi again," he said while I hurried to the refreshment table to bring something back to my box for my sister and me to eat.

I stopped in my tracks, and despite my better judgment, said, "Hi."

"You're that girl I ran over yesterday, aren't you?"

Heat flooded my cheeks as I watched the ground. "I am," I whispered.

"Again, I'm sorry about that. I was on an errand for my father. I'm certain you know how that goes."

"I do," I said aloud, surprising myself. "Fathers are quite temper driven."

"Exactly. Especially when you have mine for a father."

I couldn't help but look up at him. I'd never heard a warlock talk about their father in such a tone before. "Who's your father?"

He sighed. "The Grand Chancellor."

Immediately, I lowered my head. Just the thought of the Grand Chancellor scared me. I took a step back.

"Hey, don't go just because I mentioned my father," he said. "I'm tired of everyone running away just because of who he is."

The sorrow in his voice made me glance up at him, if only for a second.

"Please don't go," he said.

Something about him made me want to stay. Made me dare talk to him. Made me watch him through my eyelashes. "You know I have to do what you say, just because you're a warlock and I'm a woman."

He scowled, like he just tasted something bitter. "You don't have to. I mean, not if you don't want to. I wouldn't want you to have to talk to me."

I took a step closer to him. "I don't mind."

"You're different than other women."

"How so?"

"Other women wouldn't continue speaking with me. They'd keep their head down and do exactly as they're told. You're not like that."

"Is that a bad thing or a good thing?" I dared ask.

"Definitely a good thing. But why are you different?"

"I don't know. Maybe because of watching what my sister is like."

"Who's your sister?"

"Serena, Stephen's daughter."

"Ah."

Since I was being brave, I decided to go all the way. "You remember her?"

"Of course I remember her. I helped her at the ball she and Chancellor Zade held. It's where…"

I kept my voice soft. "Where your fiancée was killed?"

"Yes." He looked to the ground.

"I'm sorry for your loss." Though I wondered how much of a loss it was to him. Just a woman. Did she mean anything to him? Did he feel like he'd lost an item, or like he'd lost a person he cared about?

"Thank you." He sniffed, which I took to mean he was truly sad to see her go, though it was still hard to read exactly why. "I'm sorry she's gone, though I'm glad I was able to help your sister."

"I'm glad you helped her too. I'm not certain she would be here without you."

"I'm sure she would have found a way."

"I don't know. I was at that ball too. I saw what you did for Serena. Your assistance saved her and cost you something."

"Maybe it did." He sounded as if he was really thinking about it. As if my words actually got through to him.

It was then I realized I was being way too upfront with my words and thoughts. It was time to leave, but I didn't want to go. This was the best thing that had ever happened to me with a warlock; I'd much rather stay in his presence than have to be around another. But I couldn't stay around him forever. Besides, my sister was waiting for me.

"I should go," I said.

"I probably should too."

But both of us just stood there, waiting. For what, I wasn't sure, yet my legs didn't seem to want to move.

"Maybe I'll see you around more while we're here."

"That would be nice."

I finally left, but not without backward glances. The tournament was a good excuse to continue seeing each other. From there, our relationship just built on itself. It was the first time I ever had a relationship with a male who wasn't abusive. One who didn't hex and beat me. He earned my trust.

He's kept my trust.

The windows are done being washed. Finally. My arms and legs ache. I'm beyond ready for bed. Good thing this was my last chore for the day. I hurry to clean up and make my way to the shared bedroom.

I lie down, relieved to finally be done with my day. My eyes shut, and almost instantly, I'm asleep.

A whimper jerks me awake. Abby. She's getting upset. There

are too many others around for me to let her cry, but oh how I want to, even if for twenty minutes. I'm so exhausted.

Instead, I rock her as I drift off, hoping the motion will get her to sleep, and even more, to stay asleep. She calms and at some point, I'm finally, *finally*, able to sleep.

CHAPTER 18

The days grow longer and longer. Abby sleeps when I'm awake and wants to be awake the only time I get to rest. With my other sisters, I never had a problem like this because I could nap when they did. If I napped now, I'd probably be executed. I press on with my chores, sometimes with Tawny or another tarnished, but usually alone.

When I come to Nathaniel's room, I give him his evening tray with a half smile. He gives a full one back, but I just can't return it. There's not enough energy left in me.

I go to the water closet and fill my bucket full of water. My arms feel weak under the strain of carrying it. I press on and take it toward the window.

The bucket slips from my hand. Before it can fall to the floor, Nathaniel catches it. Only a little spills out onto the rug. He gently sets the bucket down and leads me over to a chair.

'Are you well?'

I give him a half smile. 'Just tired.'

'Are you not getting enough sleep?'

'We're only allowed five hours, and Ben doesn't like to hold still. He gets fussy when I stop moving. Because of that I often have to bounce him so he doesn't wake the others.'

'Why don't you let me take care of Ben while you lay down and get some rest?'

'I couldn't.' Though the thought is terribly appealing.

'I insist.'

Before I can protest further, he guides me to the day couch and sits me down. 'Unwrap the baby, and I'll get you a pillow and a blanket.'

There's not enough energy left in me to fight. There hasn't been enough energy in me to do much of anything. I follow his orders and have Abby unwrapped by the time he returns.

He sets a pillow and blanket beside me and reaches for the baby. Though she's all ready to go, I've never handed her over to anyone since arriving here, if I don't count Nathaniel's mother. Others have played with her, yes. But I'm the only one who has full control over her. To give her to someone else feels wrong somehow. Like I won't ever get her back.

But this is Nathaniel. I trust him with my life; I know I can trust him with my sister. I put her in his extended arms. He immediately cuddles her close, and she sighs contentedly. I can't help but feel at least a little jealous. I lie down and throw the blanket over me, but sleep doesn't want to come. All I can do is watch the two of them together. Him cooing at her and bouncing her. Her cooing back.

My eyelids grow heavy.

Next thing I know, I'm startled awake. Abby isn't next to me. I'm not in my bed in the servant's quarters. Then I remember Nathaniel offered to watch her while I slept.

He's standing by the window, looking out it, Abby nestled close to him. Asleep.

I stand and stretch, hoping I didn't sleep so long that I'm going to have a hard time getting my other chores done. Normally I'd be worrying about things like having sleep hair, especially with

Nathaniel around. I suppose being bald does have some advantages.

After taking care of the blanket and pillow, I amble my way over to him. Abby is so content in his arms. I ache deep within my gut. I will only ever have siblings, nieces, and nephews. Never will I have a child for myself. I'm too young to want one now, but someday I would have wanted one. Now I'll never even have the choice. I want to rage over it, but I calm myself and look up at Nathaniel.

His face is pale, eyes staring vacantly out the window.

'Are you well?' I spell out in front of him, in a soft blue.

The words hovering before him seem to pull him out of whatever trance he was in. He shakes himself and looks at me as the words dissipate. He gives me three very slow nods, and then looks down at Abby.

He may say he's well, but something seems to have startled him. Or maybe he's just tired, like I am. He's not used to taking care of a baby, after all, and since he managed to get her to sleep, it's likely he had to spend a lot of time bouncing her. Now he's just doing a slow rock. That's all it must be.

'I wanted to help,' he spells out before me.

'You did. Thank you.'

He shakes his head. 'The baby was wet. I changed her nappy.'

Her. He knows.

Out of all the people in the house to find out, he's the best possible choice, but no one should know at all. This not only puts him in more danger, but her as well.

'Sorry.' His spelled word is dark blue, hanging in the air. 'Also, I don't think I know how to change a nappy. I think it's on crooked.'

I hold back a laugh, some of the tension in me easing. I check her over, and sure enough, she's not even well covered. I adjust her nappy as best I can without waking her. I can't believe he even tried to change her. Most warlocks won't even come near a baby, let alone clean up after one.

This doesn't take care of the problem, though. He must see something in my gaze because he spells out, 'Don't worry. I'll keep your secret.'

Even though I knew he would, seeing the words eases the rest of that tightly wound tension inside me. He knows my biggest secret, and I trust him to keep it. I mouth, "Thank you."

'You do understand how serious this could be, though,' he spells out, yellow and green speckling his words. 'What could happen to you.'

'I don't know exactly, but I know it wouldn't be good.'

'Not good at all.' He pulls me close. Though I have to look to the side, to see what magic he's casting, it's calming being near him. 'Last time my father caught someone lying to him, he left him up in the ball room, to be tortured by a spell for a month.'

I swallow. 'That's all the more reason to make certain this secret doesn't get out.'

He grips both of my shoulders, and I turn to look in his eyes. Whatever he's feeling is intense. His gaze on me is like none I've seen before. It makes me feel like pressing myself against him and never letting go.

But it can't last forever. Not with everything I have to do. He gives a little smile and spells, 'It's time for you to go. Come back and take another nap tomorrow.'

I grin. Finding him here was the best thing that happened to me since coming to this house, in more ways than one. I nod my acceptance of more sleep. It already seems like my sanity isn't as in question as it was before. Imagine how I'd handle things if I managed more sleep.

CHAPTER 19

Three sits next to me, playing with Abby. It's still strange to refer to her as a number, but I have no other way to identify her than the three tattoos she has. I've been here long enough we almost know each other now. The routine of her playing with the baby before I go to bed and she goes back to work, happens almost every night now.

As she coos at the baby, I think maybe, just maybe, it's time to do more than spend time together. Zade's in this same house, and I haven't seen him yet. If things remain the way they are now, nothing good will ever happen. Nathaniel will still be confined to his rooms. Abby will only stay hidden as a girl for so long. And I'll die an early death, like most of the tarnished working in this house do. It's too much to hope for anything else, unless I do something about it.

But to do something about it means I'll have to break a rule. Probably more than one, by the time everything has been dealt with. I feel as if I can trust this woman, but how am I to know without giving her something that needs trusting care?

Here it goes. I cast a spell like I've been doing with Nathaniel. 'Can we talk about something?'

She immediately goes rigid. I've done it. Here's the end of all things. I'll be sacrificed by the Grand Chancellor. What must she think of me?

When she finally calms down, she sits back against the wall, face pale. But she does more than I could have hoped for. With eyes wide and face pale, she nods slowly. "Please," she mouths.

This is it. I've found someone who's not just wanting to talk but eager to do so. Eager by her *please* anyway. I should tread carefully. 'Do you know how to do magic?'

She shakes her head.

It'll be harder to teach her without talking. Plus, it'll take more energy that I don't have right now. Unless it becomes too hard, we'll have to make do with what we can. 'This is a sad place.'

Her expression seems to say, *Of course it is. Tell me something I don't know.*

'I want to make it a happy place.'

With that, she perks up. She holds up her hands and lifts her shoulders as if to say, *How?*

'I don't know how exactly, yet. Something needs to change, though.'

She nods.

'Do you think other tarnished in the house feel the same way?'

Her eyes grow serious as she nods again.

'For now, let's foster that. Help others see how things should change, but not anything that would lead to trouble.'

She shrugs. I know what she means. There's not much we can do that won't get us into trouble, except be shadows that get the work done without being noticed.

"Benjamin is so darling. Everyone loves him," she says.

She has a look in her eye that makes me think she's talking about more than just herself. Maybe Abby's a good way to reach other people's hearts. Abby is the only non-tarnished among us, though, and they think she's a baby warlock at that. Some might resent her.

86

"He is precious. I like to keep him safe next to me."

"That, I understand. He's a dear commodity. People here love babies. We haven't a lot of children around since the mistress stopped having children. Rumor is that the Grand Chancellor will soon take on a new wife. That means possibly more children, but in the mean time, we all adore having Benjamin around."

"I suppose so." Maybe it is a good idea to have Abby be a focal point. The Grand Chancellor would be less suspicious of us fawning over a warlock babe than anything else, but I don't feel comfortable putting her out there like that. The last thing she needs is more scrutiny. I should talk to Nathaniel first. See if he has any thoughts on her safety and on the tarnished working together against this.

CHAPTER 20

My days revolve entirely around seeing Nathaniel, Tawny, and Three. Everything else blurs together in a dull grey, but moments with Nathaniel are bright and warm and not nearly long enough. We enjoy the time together. We need to more than just enjoy it, though. The other tarnished seem to be discontent, and so am I. These bright spots aren't enough to get me by.

I'm in Nathaniel's room when I spell him the thought of using Abby's sweet little personality to help get the tarnished together. He's silent for longer than I like.

'I think,' he finally spells back in a dark blue, 'it's dangerous and tricky. Just look where trying to help got me. But if you're willing to take the risk, I think it's one of the best plans we could probably come up with.'

'If I'm willing to risk her.' I pace the room, but the action reminds me of Zade, so I stop. I can't not try. Even if it's risky. Just being here is a risk—one we can't negate. We may as well try to do something about it. Besides, it'll be justice to have the only child my father ever cared about for more than just money play a part in his undoing. 'I think it's a good idea. Where should I start?'

'Well, not with having anyone else change her nappy; that's certain.'

'Not unless they want to die of shock.'

We grin at each other. It feels good to have something to make light of our situation. Someone to make light of it with. 'I was thinking maybe we need to start with just getting people together as far as same opinions. Try and make sure they're against what the Grand Chancellor is doing. How he's treating women and those men he doesn't like.'

"That's a good starting point,' he spells back. 'Once you've everyone on the same page, we can start working on little things.'

'Like not having the fires magically going in the morning in the Grand Chancellor's room and the rooms he likes to spend time in.' The thought has me feeling smug.

'Maybe, but it'll be dangerous for you and anyone else who tries to go that route.'

'But what other route is there to go in?'

'Why don't we take this one step at a time and go from there? We can work on their opinions first.'

One step at a time. That sounds like something I can manage right now, in more than one aspect of my life. Working on just being friendlier with the other tarnished. Opening up their hearts. Getting them to see they have more value than the Grand Chancellor gives them. It will have to be enough. For now.

I smile at him, his grinning response warming me even down to my coldest parts. My heart that's been so neglected. Yes, I think one step at a time is the way it should be.

CHAPTER 21

I wake to chaos in the house. Everyone frantically moves from place to place, carrying flowers or cleaning something. Judging from the disorder, the kitchens are probably even more hectic. I stop when I find Three. She seems to get even less sleep than I do.

"What is all this running about for?"

"Time to prepare for a wedding celebration," she says.

"It's true, then? The Grand Chancellor is really taking a second wife?" I ask.

"He certainly is. And hosting the wedding party here afterward for all his friends."

More like all his law officers, or people who are too scared of him to do anything else. "Do you know who he's marrying?"

"Some girl named Nelly, Sam's daughter."

I gasp. It can't be Annabelle's friend, whom Waverly saved from the attacking law officers. Can it? I never did know what happened to her after the battle. Maybe she didn't get caught right away, but later on. She did have a lot of magic in her blood. Magic the Grand Chancellor would be sure to want.

"Is she someone you know?" Three asks.

90

I suppose we'll soon find out.

* * *

WE SPEND the next two weeks working like crazy to get the house ready. We're allowed even less sleep than we usually get, but thankfully I can still nap at Nathaniel's. Unfortunately, I can't spend as much time there as before because the rest of the house needs more attention.

The house looks good when we finish, though a little gaudy for my tastes. It's lavish with its decorations, though so different from what Waverly described from Envado. There, everything would be spelled. Here, everything is an actual physical decoration. Fabric draped across the stair railings. Flowers hung or in vases all around. Chandeliers with electric light, which are usually left off, are on.

The wedding ceremony was completed yesterday, and now we're serving the after celebration. The Grand Chancellor has more *friends* than I expected. No wonder he's still ruling this country, despite his poor treatment of everyone. How will we ever come close to taking him out of power? The house is packed with people, everywhere except the servants' area and Nathaniel's rooms. That's too many supporters. Not to mention his massive amount of power. We're doomed.

But for some crazy reason, we're going to try anyway. Maybe we'll at least be able to find a way to be more at peace with our situation.

I'm told Nathaniel isn't feeling well today, and he's attended by a magical physician. More like his father won't allow him out, even for something as grand as this.

Abby and I are with father this evening. We have to follow him everywhere so he can show her off. It makes me laugh on the inside to know he's showing off a daughter. Other than the amusement I get from his mistake, it's a long, boring night. Until I see the Grand Chancellor's new wife, sitting at his feet. The collar around her throat makes me want to retch. It's Nelly, Annabelle's friend. The one who hated Waverly at first, but practically worshiped the ground she walked on after Waverly saved her life.

Whether this is good or bad, I'm uncertain. It's definitely bad for her, but part of me wonders if it may be good for us. If there's something she'll be able and willing to do to improve our chances of defeating the Grand Chancellor, or at the very least, to help us out of here.

Thankfully, father heads toward her and the Grand Chancellor, so I'll get a better glance at her. Maybe she'll see me too, though it's unlikely. Not since I became a tarnished. The only two people who see me that aren't tarnished are Abby and Nathaniel. Nelly probably wouldn't recognize me as I am now.

And I'm right. I stand next to her, and her gaze passes right over me, as if I'm not even here. I believed I'd gotten over being overlooked, but now I think there's much more left for me to handle. Seeing someone who should know me personally and doesn't changes everything.

I feel the way they want me to—less than a person. Less than a shadow.

Father shows off Abby, and it's like she's hovering in the middle of the air. By herself. Or maybe they think a shadow is holding her up.

Later, perhaps, will be a better time to see if Nelly remembers who I am. If she's willing to help. For now, father sends me and the baby away with a flick of his wrist. Now that he's shown off what he thinks is his own little warlock to the Grand Chancellor, he's done with us for the night. Thank goodness.

I'd say hi to Tawny, but she's stuck in the kitchens for the night. I know if I go there, not only will she not be able to talk, but I'll be put to work. I make my way through the crowd with Abby, heading toward our rooms. Suddenly, there's a warlock walking beside me. This isn't unusual, as the place is so crowded, you can't not be by someone. The unusual part is that he speaks. To me.

"Are you Bethany?" he whispers.

The sound of my name, something the Grand Chancellor says I no longer own even though I know it's still mine, is heartening. Still, I'm not supposed to talk. Instead, I nod.

"Your sisters and mother all made it safely to Envado."

That statement makes me focus all my willpower on taking the next step. On moving forward and acting as if everything is well and normal, when it's anything but.

My whole being wants to shout out. I want to celebrate this elation that makes me feel as if I'm floating far above the crowd. But of course, I remain expressionless.

He slips me a small piece of paper. "Destroy it as soon as possible."

With that, he's gone. Lost in the crowd that's overwhelming me. First things first. I have to get somewhere I can read the paper. The only place that's truly private at a time like this. The water closet.

I hurry, moving through walls of people, the maze-like corridors, and out the servants' entrance to the outhouse. Thankfully, no one is using it, and no one is around. They're all too busy with their duties at the ball. I'm grateful my only duty tonight is taking care of Abby so I'm able to do this.

I hurry in and close the door behind me. I almost tear the paper in my haste to get it open. Inside it reads,

EVERYONE IS ALIVE AND WELL. *We miss and worry for you. Sanos is not lost. We carry on, despite everything. We are working on getting you out. Leave us notes in the back, by the door. Behind the third brick to the right.*

. . .

THEY REALLY ARE alive and well. They and the rebel group, Sanos. There's nothing that can harm them, now they're out of Chardonia. At least nothing that can harm them physically. With everything going on here, I'm sure they're hurting emotionally.

I tear the piece of paper as small as I can. Then I chance the one thing I try to keep to a minimum except when I'm talking with Nathaniel. I cast a spell, a fire one that leaves the paper in ashes. Then I throw those ashes down with the smelling refuse. Hopefully, that's good enough.

And now I have a way to contact the outside world. I don't know who it was that passed me the note, but whoever it was means the rebel group is still up and running, hopefully with Waverly and Jack still helping out. The two of them helped more with the war than anyone else I know. It'd be a shame if their talents went to waste just because we lost before.

But none of that matters right now because my family is alive, well, and safe. I feel as if I'm the star of the party the rest of the night, even if no one gives me a second glance.

CHAPTER 22

The next morning, I burst into Nathaniel's room, unable to contain my excitement. As soon as I'm certain he's alone, I spell out, 'There's been a message from Serena.'

'Is she well?'

'She, my other siblings, and my mother are all safe in Envado.'

His expression brightens. 'Wonderful news!'

'Yes. And I have instructions on how to contact her. Our plan doesn't just have to be with the tarnished in this house. We can work with those on the outside as well.'

He grins at me, and I grin back.

'Sanos must have made it through your father's purge. Someone handed me the note at the wedding.'

'Now if only we knew what to do with the opportunity. We'll think of something, or maybe they will and will contact us again. In the meantime, I'm happy you are able to contact your sister.'

'There's something else.' I spell out.

'What is it?'

'One of the girls who helped with our rebellion is your father's new wife.'

He sits back, as if trying to absorb this news. 'Does she know who you are?'

'She didn't seem to recognize me at the party last night. I'm to clean her room after I do yours this morning. If she's there, I don't know if I should try and get her to remember me or not.'

'It could be risky.'

'But it could also mean a better insight into what your father has planned.'

He rests his chin on his hand. 'Perhaps. But he wouldn't just give a woman information.'

'But he wouldn't stop himself from talking about things around her. Would he?'

Nathaniel shrugs. 'It's hard to say. I think he knows women are smarter than he tries to convince everyone they are, but he also doesn't value them at all.'

'So we may or may not get information from her, if she's willing to help. Do you think it's worth the risk?'

He's quiet a moment, as I rock Abby back to sleep.

'Yes. I think it is worth the risk.' He grabs my hand, which sends a wave of happiness through me. 'But please be careful. I don't want anything bad to happen to you.'

My heart warms, and I want to move closer to him. So I do. We stand together, like we're the only people left in the world.

If only it were so.

I SLIP inside Nelly's room, hoping she'll be here. When I glance around the room, there's no one. Stifling my disappointment, I get to work, starting with scrubbing the water closet. May as well get the worst job out of the way. Though her toilet is flushable. So much more pleasant to be around than the one for the tarnished.

Once that job is taken care of, I make the bed and get to dusting. It's while I'm dusting the table with the Woman's Canon on it that the door opens. I look out of the corner of my eye to discover it's Nelly. My heart soars a moment until I realize she's not alone. The Grand Chancellor is with her. I want to recoil. To go back and hide in the water closet.

As he leans in for a kiss, I hurry to glance anywhere but at them. Gross. I can't imagine having to kiss him. My stomach is sick just thinking about it. *Ew.*

"I expect to see you at dinner," he says and then leaves, shutting the door behind him.

Thank goodness he's gone. I don't think my nerves or my stomach could handle his presence any longer.

I continue my work as Nelly flings herself on the bed. I pretend harder than ever to be invisible. Now doesn't seem the best of times to reintroduce myself to her.

Then she starts crying. I stare at her prone form, face down, sobbing into her pillow. Hoping it won't cost my life, I inch forward until I reach her. Slowly, ever so slowly, I reach my hand out and gently pat her back.

She jumps up and scowls, but then she sees me. As soon as our gazes meet, her splotched face goes from angry to curious. The longer we stare at each other, the more the redness fades from her face.

She starts to say something, but I hurry to put a finger to my lips to shush her. I cup my hand around my ear and point to the wall, just as Three did when I first arrived. Nelly seems to understand the message and doesn't say anything. By the way she bites her lip, I know she's dying to. Dare I risk spelling a message out to her? I have to; otherwise we'll never communicate enough to get the information we need about the Grand Chancellor.

Here it is. The moment she either sends me to the Grand Chancellor for punishment, or she joins our side. I spell out, 'I'm sorry.'

She stares at the spell, a soft green hovering before her eyes in glowing lights. The longer she stares, the more her expression turns from shocked to determined. And then she does exactly what I was hoping she would do. She spells a message back, caked with blue. 'Sorry about what?'

'Sorry you're sad. Sorry you're in this position. Sorry I can't do more for you.'

She stares at me more, as if trying to figure something out. 'Do I know you from somewhere?"'

It's good to have a hint of recognition in there, but it makes me wonder even more how Nathaniel recognized me so readily. 'Yes, you do. I'm Bethany. Serena and Cynthia's sister.'

'Bethany. What are you doing here? When did you become tarnished? What happened to your sisters?'

I sigh, wishing I could forget the whole thing instead of having to rehash it again. 'It's a long story.'

'I have all the time in the world until dinner.'

'Unfortunately, I don't. I need to clean your room and get on with my other chores. But I can tell you as I clean.'

I recap my story as best I can without getting too emotional, while I clean her room. She reads my spelled words with rapt attention, stopping me on occasion to clarify one point or another. I'm very careful at what I tell her, though. And while I do tell her this is Stephen's child I'm taking care of, I also make sure to say Abby is a boy. Nathaniel is already one person more than I planned on telling.

When I finish, she spells out, 'I would like to help. The Grand Chancellor is… not someone I'd like to see stay in power.'

Or stay with her, if I had to guess. 'Thank you. Any information you can give me would be valuable beyond measure.'

'I will do what I can.'

'I have to go now. There'll be trouble if I don't finish my duties.'

'Of course. I hope to see you soon.'

'They are talking of switching around who cleans your rooms, and sometimes I may have another person with me, but I'll try to speak with you when possible. In the mean time, keep safe.'

'You as well.'

As if that's a possibility in this house.

CHAPTER 23

I t's my turn to clean the Grand Chancellor's room. Not a task I've been looking forward to ever since I was introduced to it. The only upside is he's out of the house today, so the likelihood of him coming into his rooms while I'm cleaning is very small.

I enter through the servants' door and get to work. As I dust, the books call my attention. I've always loved books, but only ever being able to read the Woman's Canon until Serena gained ownership of us hasn't provided much opportunity. Now I can't even read the Woman's Cannon. As a tarnished, I can't read at all.

The books call to me. I want to at least know what they are. I glance around the room, even though I know I'm alone. There's no colored spell over them. Nothing to stop me from taking a look if I put them back exactly as they were when I'm done.

I touch a book at random. Number thirteen. I hold my breath and pull it out in one swift motion. Nothing happens. I didn't think there was a spell, but I don't know for certain. I open the book to find a thin, sprawling handwriting. It appears to be a journal of some sort. The Grand Chancellor's.

I look across over sixty volumes. He is obsessed with keeping a record of himself.

It reads,

I saw Julia today. She was more beautiful than ever. I want to lock her up in my house, where no other man can look at her. I want to own her. Unfortunately, she was walking with another man. Chancellor Jacob. What I wouldn't give to have him out of the picture. He gets in my way too much, with politics and now with Julia.

Nothing shall stand in my way of gaining her. Nothing.

I don't know who Julia is, but Chancellor Jacob was the man Thomas defeated and whose possessions he won, only to be thwarted by Zade who won Serena. I know Julia wasn't around then. I wonder what happened with her. If the Grand Chancellor ever owned her.

I've been spurned. Julia says she hates me and will never be with me. She's to marry another. Jacob. I loved her, and she spurned me. Now I choose not to love. Now I choose to make women what they should be.

Women have always been a thorn in my side. One I've tried to pull out, but I see I'll have to smash them apart to get anywhere with them. If only they weren't such fickle creatures. Soon they'll be fixed up. Soon.

The words make me shiver. I snap the book closed. Now I know at least part of the reason women have become so mistreated. But what am I doing, reading the writings of a madman?

And yet, curiosity stirs within me. How did he get to be the Grand Chancellor? And what other information is contained in these books that could help me know more about him? Help maybe find a way to overcome him?

Whatever I'm to read, I must do it fast. There isn't much time left before I'll be missed, and who's to say when I'll have this chance again?

I slip the book back into the case and pull out another, higher numbered one, and open to a random page.

I'M BEGINNING to suspect there are more changes taking place than just my magic being increased by so many sacrifices. I sleep less and less after each sacrifice. Food no longer holds the same appeal it once did. I'm changing, but into what, I'm uncertain.

THE THOUGHT GIVES ME CHILLS. If he sleeps little and doesn't care about food, how human can he be? I place the book down right where it belongs. This is something I have to pass along to Sanos. I don't know what use it will be, but it seems like something they need to know. I put my hand on my duster. I want to read more, to understand what he means, but I have to work.

"What do you think you're doing?" Fredrick says behind me, startling me.

Did he see me? Am I caught? Why type of punishment will they dole out? Just how much trouble am I in? And does it matter if they're going to execute me anyway?

"Answer me, tarnished!"

"I am just finishing cleaning up." I hope my voice isn't as shaky as it feels.

"Likely story. Get up."

He knows then. That's it. Punishment is coming. How bad will it be? It can't be as bad as my death. At least I don't think they would kill me now, not when they are planning on sacrificing me for the tournament. Then again, maybe death is preferable to whatever they have planned for me.

As soon as I stand, he smacks me across the face and sends me sprawling to the ground. I touch my cheek, surprised at such force. It's been too long since father hit me. I forgot how bad it can sting. How much worse it hurts the inside of me than the outside.

Abby is safely tucked inside her pouch, thank goodness. I don't know how much I could contain myself if he did something to hurt her.

"Get up, wench."

I struggle to my feet, making certain to keep my distance from him. It doesn't work. He crosses the bit of distance to me and smacks me across the face again. This time I taste blood.

"Tsk, tsk. You got blood on the Grand Chancellor's carpet. Best clean that up before he gets here, which I heard is going to be soon. You don't want to know what he did to the last tarnished he found still cleaning when he got home."

He turns and leaves the room through the servants' entrance. Does that mean he saw me looking at the Grand Chancellor's books or not? I'm inclined to think not. Had he, the punishment would likely have been more severe.

I glance down at the floor. Sure enough, there are several spots of blood. More of it is dripping. I grab a cloth and press it to my lip to keep any more from marring the perfectly white carpet.

How soon is the Grand Chancellor going to be back? Fredrick was right about one thing. I most definitely don't want to be here when the Grand Chancellor arrives. I bend down, grab a rag, and with my free hand, I start scrubbing. Instead of coming out, it just smears. I dab at it instead. Some of the red comes out, but not nearly enough.

No one's here. I want to use magic to fix it, but I feel like I'm being watched. Why, I'm uncertain, but I don't dare use magic because of it.

I take the cloth away from my face. The bleeding seems to have stopped, or at least slowed. I dunk my other rag in a bucket of soapy water, wring it out, and dab back at the red spots. They fade more and more, but it takes time. Too much time. The Grand Chancellor could be walking in at any moment.

What if I left now? The stains are just a few, small pink dots. He'll notice them, though. Just look how clean his room is. Everything is pristine. I don't know how he would not notice.

My hand shakes as I continue to dab at the stains, fear making my hand unsteady. I glance around and finally see why I felt like I was being watched. Fredrick didn't leave. Not entirely. He's watching me from just inside the servants' entrance.

My gaze meets his.

He scoffs at me. "Can't do it, can you? Guess you're going to be in trouble with the Grand Chancellor."

With that, he leaves my sight. After a moment, I get up on shaky legs and move to the servants' entrance. No one is there. He's really gone this time.

Relief fills me. I can get it out with magic. There will be no consequences. I can do this. Just as I move to the spot, I hear a door close from the outer room. *No.* The Grand Chancellor has returned.

I rush to cast spells over the spots, pulling the last of the red from the carpet to my bucket. I grab my bucket, rags, and duster. As I cross the vast room, I think there's not going to be enough time. What will the Grand Chancellor do to me? Will he save me since I'm supposed to be sacrificed at the tournament? Will he torture me? Will he even realize I'm the one supposed to be sacrificed?

Abby stirs. She can't wake, not now!

Fear makes me quake as the handle to the door turns. I run the last few steps, making it into the servants' entrance as the door opens. I made it in, but I still have to close the door. As quietly as I can, I set my bucket down.

While I rock Abby to keep her quiet, I start closing the door slowly. The Grand Chancellor comes into view, his back toward me. I hold my breath. The door squeaks. The Grand Chancellor Stops. I don't move. I don't breath. I don't do anything.

My heart pounds in my chest. I worry he'll know I'm here just from the sound it makes. But no, he takes a step forward. And another. I ease the door all the way closed, but don't latch it. Even if I'm supposed to close it all the way, I don't dare let it make that clicking sound.

I pick up my bucket and inch away, trying to keep my steps silent. I hurry away, grateful my life is still intact and I have nothing worse than a split lip.

CHAPTER 24

'What happened?' Nathaniel spells as soon as I enter his room with my cleaning supplies.

I swallow, my fear coming back at the memory of what took place. I start shaking. He takes my cleaning supplies and places them on the floor. He reaches for my hand. As soon as we make contact, my fear eases behind his comfort. Just that small contact is a soothing balm to my soul. I want to lean into him. To let myself be held by him.

But that's rather forward. Even if I care about him a great deal and we hugged when I first got here, I shouldn't press myself against him any time I feel like it. For now, just holding his hand is enough. It's a type of contact I've always wanted, and I'm grateful to have it now, when things are harder than ever.

'Bethany? What's going on?' The anxiety wrinkling his face pulls me back together.

'Do you know Fredrick?'

'Of course it was him.' Nathaniel forms his other hand into a fist. 'He's the biggest bully. Which is why my father put him in charge of the tarnished. I think he's caused more tarnished to be killed than any other person on this estate.'

His words make me feel vaguely ill and remind me of just how close I came to serious punishment. 'I saw your father. Or his back, anyway. I almost didn't get out of his room in time.'

'You're shaking.' He takes hold of my free hand, making it so it's more difficult to spell out messages, but it's worth it. I squeeze both his hands, wishing that as much as they make me feel good, they could actually fix all the problems in the world. They feel as if they have that power.

Once my shaking stops, he lets go of one of my hands, and the loss is immediate. 'What happened with my father?' he asks.

I spell to him everything I learned and then the fact that I almost got caught.

'I'm glad you made it out safely.'

'Me too.' I squeeze his hand, needing the reassurance. 'Did you know this about your father?'

'No. I knew he hates women of course, but I didn't know he became more resentful after an issue with one. I didn't know he was even capable of wanting a specific woman for more than just her blood.'

I shiver. 'Whatever he wants one for, it gives me the creeps.'

'Honestly, me too.' He's silent a moment and then adds, 'I had no idea he doesn't need much food or sleep.'

'What do you make of it?'

He sits a moment. 'I don't know exactly. It doesn't sound good. You should send a message to your sisters about what you learned.'

'I will. I only hope they can do something with the information.' I wish I could do something with it. Something to make a difference.

CHAPTER 25

After I put Abby on the floor to play, I stretch and rub my back. "The job's hard on a person's body," Three says. "It helps if you stretch before you start work, and if you do so again several times throughout the day."

I look at her closer than I have before. She must be at least fifty now, though it's hard to tell without hair going gray and tattoos across her face. I can't imagine doing this for thirty or more years. Of course, I won't have to. I'll be dead long before then.

"Does it bother you, working here?"

"When you do something for so long, it almost doesn't matter anymore." She shrugs. "Besides, it's not a bad life. I have shelter and food. Tarnished are rarely beaten or hexed because we're not even considered people anymore. Tarnished are almost like magic. We get things done without anyone even noticing."

"But that means we don't get noticed for anything good, either. Doesn't that ever bother you?"

"When you've lived this life as long as I have, it just that. Life."

How depressing. It makes my imminent death seem almost appealing.

"You look tired," she says.

I shrug. "I'm allowed as much sleep as everyone else, only Benjamin here likes to be moving. As soon as I try to go to bed, he starts fussing."

"I don't mind watching him for a while right now, if you want to try to get some sleep."

"You don't need to do that. You get little sleep as well."

"Yes, but I'm used to it. I enjoy the baby more than I enjoy sleep anyway. He's a breath of fresh air around this place."

"If you're sure." I did just change Abby's nappy, so she should be fine

"Go on. I'll wake you in a while."

With many thanks, I leave the room and hurry to my bed. Unfortunately, without Abby, it's hard to sleep. I can't manage to shut my eyes without worrying about her. How she's behaving and if she's safe. After what feels like too long a time, I decide I just can't do it. I want to, I desperately need to, but Abby's safety has become my life. Without her, I'm not comfortable enough to sleep. At least I got some rest, as fitful as it may have been.

I stand and hurry back to the room. Only before I can get there, another tarnished stops me. "There's been a spill in the kitchen. You're needed to help clean it."

Of course I am. I hesitate for just a moment, wondering if I should get Abby before heading to clean it up. It hasn't been that long, though, and Three did say how much she enjoyed time with the baby. It will be nice to not have Abby's weight added to me as I complete the chore. I'll hurry through it as fast as I can and then return to get her.

The spill ends up being a stack of plates, shards everywhere. I and several other tarnished hurry to clean them up so no one gets cut. The job takes a little longer than I expected but still not as long as I could have been sleeping.

"Thank you for your help," the head cook says. "Why don't you sit a moment and have some tea? You should be on your break anyway, and it is very soothing."

"That's very kind of you." And I do have time. Abby is in good hands. "I would like some. Thank you."

He gets me a cup and hustles back to his work. "Where is that baby boy you always carry around?"

"He's being watched by the woman with three slashes across her nose."

"That's kind of her."

"Yes, it is." I'm finding most of these tarnished are full of kindness, just like Katherine. I wonder how the circumstances don't make them bitter, like they want to make me. Though I suppose a bitter tarnished wouldn't survive very long in this world. They would be more likely to make a mistake, and mistakes can't happen when you're a tarnished. Not if you want to stay alive.

As I drink my tea, which is very relaxing, I talk to the cook. He's kind—that was easy enough to figure out the first day I was here—but there's more to him as well. I just wish we could speak without worrying about being overheard. Fear always changes what would be said.

Once finished, I give my thanks and goodbyes, and I hurry back to the room we always relax in. When I open the door, Three's face is ashen. I hurry to close the door. What in Chardonia could have caused her to look so fretful? Abby is happily kicking on the floor, trying to roll her tiny body but not quite making it.

"Are you well?" I ask.

She shakes her head but says, "Of course. Benjamin was sweet. He just had a messy nappy." My heart sinks even before she continues. "I changed it for you."

"You didn't have to do that," I say while on the inside I'm screaming at myself. She should have never had a messy nappy. I took care of it before I left. Why did I ever leave her alone? Why?

"I'm sorry. I was just trying to be helpful," she says.

"I know." I spell out, 'But we have to keep it a secret.'

She nods and puts her hand to her heart. "He's such a dear little boy. I'm so glad you let me have some time with him."

I let out a breath and hope she means as well as she says. Knowing Abby's gender could be big for her. She told me before how she's lived most of her life under these horrid conditions. Something as huge as this could change it for her. At least get her some more sleep. Then again, maybe I'm overestimating how much my father would care to give a tarnished a reward.

"I'm happy to have your help," I fib.

"Did you get some rest?"

"I tried." And shouldn't have bothered. "But I couldn't sleep without Ben trying to keep me awake."

She laughs. "That sounds like quite the problem."

For the first time since I enter the room, I smile. "Very much. I would have been back sooner, but there were some broken dishes in the kitchen."

"That's fine. I hope you enjoyed your break and know that I treasured the time myself. I dearly love this little one."

I give a sigh of relief. She does love Abby. That's plain to see. I only hope the secret can stay just that. Secret.

CHAPTER 26

I'm cleaning Nelly's room, a job that I don't mind so much. It's not as good as taking care of Nathaniel's room, but it's not nearly as bad as being around Fredrick. Nelly is almost always here, and though she doesn't talk or spell to me much, it's nice to be around someone I remember from before.

I'm halfway done cleaning when she spells out, 'You're lucky Benjamin was caught with you instead of Abigail.'

Just the subject I don't want to talk about. 'Yes, very fortunate.'

'You said the others are safe. Is there any way to find out if my family is safe as well?'

I haven't told her how easy it is for me to communicate with the outside yet. I know she's trustworthy, but it's like telling everyone Abby is a girl. The more people who know, the more dangerous it is, especially when she's the Grand Chancellor's wife. And she hasn't brought us any information we didn't already know.

I want to fall back on a bed and never get out of it. We're getting nowhere with trying to help. Yes, the other tarnished are becoming more discontent with their lot in life, but without anything to do about it, it feels more like a disservice than something helpful.

This is too hard to not give away too much information while still trying to remain honest. It's too exhausting to keep up with. 'There may be a way to find out if your family is safe. It will take some time, though.'

'I can handle time. I can't handle not knowing.'

'I'll do my best.' Though for me it's just putting a note in its place. Cynthia and the others will have to do the hard work, finding out the information Nelly wants.

"How are you liking your new position as the Grand Chancellor's wife?" I know I shouldn't talk to her, but I want to see what she says when she knows he might be listening.

"He's… very generous," she says, and then spells out, 'At least he doesn't hex me too often yet.'

"That's good." And very much surprising. Maybe he is too busy to worry about punishments for his new wife?

"He's told me all about the tournament and the box I'll be allowed to sit in." She puts a hand over her mouth like she said something she shouldn't, her gaze going to my neck. "I'm so sorry. I shouldn't bring up the tournament."

"It's what's to be." Or not, if there's anything I can do to stop the Grand Chancellor. If I'm going to die anyway, what's from stopping me to do whatever I can to thwart him?

"You have a good attitude about it."

"I'm a tarnished. We are less than shadows that do what we are told. Nothing more."

'I'm so sorry,' she spells out. 'I wish there was something I could do to change it.'

'Maybe…' I have to chance this. 'If you could work hard at getting information from the Grand Chancellor for us. Any information at all that could help us. Just maybe there'll be something I'll be able to do. Some way to get out of it.'

'Of course I will. I've be trying my best.'

I breathe a sigh of relief. 'Thank you. I appreciate it.'

Now if only there was a way to make her best be enough to save not just my life, but also thousands of others, by getting rid of the Grand Chancellor.

As soon as I'm alone that night, I send a note out to Cynthia, telling her about Nelly and asking about her family. There's something about this that has a chill racing through me. So much so, I almost hate to send it. It's probably just nerves and the cool night air. I send it off.

After all this time without contact, it's hard to think this paper will really make it to them. Maybe it will get lost in some abyss. Or worse yet, captured by someone sympathetic to the Grand Chancellor.

The thought haunts me as I return to my room. I wish I could discuss it with Nathaniel. Talking to him always eases my worries. Tomorrow morning I'll see him. Not until I've been awake several hours, but it's not that far away. It will have to be enough.

Waverly

CHAPTER 27

My legs shake as I make my way toward the Queen. I've never felt such nerves in her presence before, but then I've never brought the type of news I'm bringing today.

The Queen is sedate today. Not a lot of the flash and glam that usually surrounds her in more public settings. In fact, there doesn't seem to be a single spell around her. Her face is pale and drawn. I suppose having one of your children lost is reason enough to be like that. I know having my brother in a dungeon and two of my best friends in the Grand Chancellor's house makes me sick. At least we know where Tawny is now.

"You bring me news?" The Queen's voice is calm and stately, belying what turmoil must be filling her at this moment.

I curtsy to her. "I do. Tawny is alive."

She closes her eyes and lets out a gasp of air. "Tell me everything you know."

"It's not as bad as it could be, but I'm afraid it's not good either. She's been tarnished."

The Queen's hand goes to her throat. I can't imagine what she must be feeling. Her daughter, third in line for the throne of Envado, has been treated inhumanely. And to top it off, will never have children. Of course, that's only if we can get her back from Chardonia before something worse happens to her.

"We must go to war this minute." The Queen stands.

I've been dismissed, but I hurry after her, hoping she forgives me. "Your Highness, please excuse me, but I don't think we should go to war."

She turns on me, anger flaming her eyes. "What do you mean? I thought Tawny was your friend."

"She is. And I didn't mean we shouldn't get her back. I just mean I don't think we should go to war yet."

"Why ever not?"

"My friend in the Grand Chancellor's house has been giving us information. It seems the Grand Chancellor is even more than we thought. Besides just being stronger than even we can imagine, he's stopped doing normal things like sleeping and eating. I don't think this is someone we can jump into a fight against without more information and a good plan in place."

"You think I shouldn't go after my daughter?"

"I think you should go after your daughter when we're certain you'll get her back. I've already messed up a war against the Grand Chancellor once. I don't think we should underestimate him again."

She thinks about this a moment before giving me her full attention. "What do you think we should do?"

"We should definitely go to war. Just not yet. First, we need to gain more information." As I lay my idea forth, light dawns on her face.

Bethany

CHAPTER 28

It's visitors' day. I've never served at one until today. I'm curious to see what it's like, but it means I only have time to take Nathaniel his tray before I have to hurry away. There's so much I want to say to him. I wish there was time to say it. New circumstances are still a good change of pace. I've wondered who visits the Grand Chancellor, and now I get to find out.

Cook loads me with two trays of food. I hurry to the main sitting room, the one where the Grand Chancellor and father sat in when I first arrived. That moment seems like so long ago. It's hard to remember a life before this one. It seems as if I've always worked here.

Once I get to the sitting room, another tarnished opens the door for me and I move in. I set the trays down on the table between several men and hurry to the spot I'm supposed to wait. It's near the center of the room, close to where the men are, but hidden back in the shadows of the curtains.

Once situated, I take the time to see who's here. The Grand Chancellor, of course, and father. He doesn't seem to care I'm here, that I'm gently rocking his *son* to keep him quiet. It's like, as much as he always wanted a son, he still can't be bothered with anything other than himself.

There are also several law officers here and my father. None of the people I would willingly put myself by.

They eat and smoke as if the entire world belongs to them and they're enjoying the spoils. It's disgusting to watch them shove food in their mouth like the pigs they are. I leave two more times to bring back trays laden with food.

It's like they don't even notice I'm the one bringing the food, and the food just magically appears before them. Except the Grand Chancellor. His gaze is shrewd, taking in even us tarnished when no one else seems to observe us. I never realized before how carefully he watches a room. How he takes in everything and everyone.

He also doesn't eat or smoke, just sits back while everyone else enjoys those pleasures. Why would he provide so much of people's wants and not partake himself?

He's so strange. Extra clean. Harsh, even to his own son. Doesn't eat of what others around him do.

"Women," a law officer says. "They're a right pain. I can't wait until my house is clear of them. They are a bother to even punish."

"Watch your mouth," the Grand Chancellor says. "They may be a pain, but they're needed. Without their magic, our world would fall apart."

"You certainly don't need them," my father says. And I don't know why. Guess he should have learned when to keep his mouth shut like he taught his daughters to all these years.

"Certainly so. Do any of you even understand how much we rely on women's magic? It's needed. We've not only had to take magic from women, but now from our lower class too. My house wouldn't have electricity without them. If you don't like it, then you should join Chryos. They get their electricity from coal."

"Surely things aren't as necessary as all that," the first law officer says.

The Grand Chancellor goes deathly still. Not for the first time, I'm grateful to be considered less than a shadow.

"Let's use you as a source of one for my power plants and see if you still feel the same way." The Grand Chancellor snaps his fingers, and the other law officers quickly move to him.

"I didn't mean it," the man who doubted him hollers. "I'm just learning."

"And you're going somewhere you can learn." The Grand Chancellor motions for the warlocks to take the man away.

With my eyes lowered, I watch as they drag him from the room. The Grand Chancellor just created another person more likely to be on our side.

CHAPTER 29

I finish my chores a little early and enter Nathaniel's room, excited to get an early start on the best part of my day. I find him on the floor doing pushups.

As soon as he sees me, he jumps to his feet, sweet beading his forehead. 'You're here early.'

'You're exercising.'

'It keeps some of the boredom away.'

I eye his new muscles with appreciation. No wonder he's gotten so strong.

After setting down my cleaning supplies, I get to work with him at my side. It's so much nicer when I have to clean with him than anyone else.

'Tell me more about your father,' I say.

'Like what?'

'Like why he is the way he is. More than what I learned in the journals.'

'If I knew that, I'd be more likely to get us out of this predicament. I don't understand him. I don't think anyone really does.'

That's disheartening. There has to be something that can help. 'What you do know about him?'

'He's obsessed with power and lowering those around him. Women, obviously, but even men with lesser power are tarnished. He has plans to put to death not just Zade but also Councilman Daniel, a Chardonian man. Anyone who shows even the slightest rebellion is punished in some way.'

I never told him about my planned demise at the upcoming tournament. I wonder if he knows why I am marked for death. How should I tell him? It's now I realize that despite all our talks, we never speak. There is no telling him. Just writing it. May as well get it over with.

'He has plans for me at the tournament as well. I'm to be sacrificed.'

"No." Nathaniel drops his rag, which falls to the floor with a mess of water.

He didn't just say that out loud. We have to keep quiet. I must have shocked him badly. It wasn't my intention. I take a deep breath, trying to steel myself. To have strength when all I feel is weakness.

'It's true,' I spell. 'I'm afraid your father wants to make an example of me since I was part of the rebellion group.'

He puts his head in his hands. 'No one is safe. Not even the woman I…'

I shake my head. 'Most likely he wants my magic as well. Though I was never tested, my sisters proved very strong. Cynthia is the strongest woman in quite some time. It's no surprise he wants to add me to his collection.'

Nathaniel says nothing. He just sits there, staring at me with profound sadness. Finally, he glances away, tears forming in his eyes. He brushes them away before they fall and then grabs onto my arm. The connection is enough to make my own eyes fill with tears, but I don't feel like crying. Not when I've been so strong for so long. I'm certain I'll cry sometime, but now I just want to enjoy him.

I give him a small smile. 'Your rag is making a mess.'

He looks down and cocks an eyebrow. 'So it is.' He picks up the rag and grabs a dry one to mop the wetness left behind on the carpet. When he's partway through, he stops and looks at me. 'I'll do everything in my power to change your fate.'

I swallow past the thickening in my throat. It seems to happen all too much lately. 'I wish you could, but there's nothing to be done about it. At least nothing I can think of.'

'We'll work on it. There has to be some way to save you.'

'Your father is a very powerful, shrewd man. I believe he's thought of everything.'

'He may be powerful and shrewd, but he's not perfect. We'll find something.'

I hope he's right, but I expect to be sacrificed at the tournament.

CHAPTER 30

It takes too much time for a response to my note about Nelly. Though it's only a short while, it feels like months. It's too important a question for the reply to take this long. Though I should just be grateful to get one at all.

I grab the note from behind the third brick to the right and hurry to put the brick back before anyone sees. I make my way to the outhouse, knowing it's not just the best place for privacy but the only place. My fingers tremble as I open the note.

Miss you. Sorry to say Nelly's family is dead. Protect T at all costs. We'll be coming for you.

How can they be coming for me? Even if they found more help in Envado, the Grand Chancellor is strong. Too strong. It would take everyone in both nations to be able to defeat him. There's no hope for this.

But these thoughts prevent me from thinking about Nelly. I don't want to. I can't. How is she going to react when she finds out her family is dead? How did they die? I wish I had more information for her. Something to give her hope or peace. But this… I just know her family is dead. How will I be able to tell her?

And what does it mean, protect Tawny at all costs? It makes it seem like she's someone important. Someone the Envadi can't live without. Someone harboring a secret, like I suspected.

If this is the case, they're in for a big shock when they discover she is a tarnished. I'll do my best to help keep her safe. I don't know how much I can do under these circumstances, though. We're both prisoners of the most powerful mad man in the world. How can I possibly protect her from him? I can only hope the new idea I have blossoms into something enough to keep us all safe.

CHAPTER 31

When I last spoke with Nelly, it gave me an idea about
something we could try on the Grand Chancellor. The
problem is it's not only risky but downright dangerous.

I should talk to Nathaniel about this. He has to know eventually if we're going to go through with it, but I can't bring myself to
tell him I have a plan to kill his father. No matter how much
Nathaniel thinks he hates him, he's still his father. Instead, I have
to ask Three. I don't know who else to turn to. I have to hope she's
the right person to turn to.

'What if...' I don't know if I can bring myself to spell the rest
out to Three. If this works, the war with the Grand Chancellor
will be over in no time. But if it fails, the consequences will
be dire.

Three prods, writing on a scrap of paper. *What is it?*

'It would be dangerous.'

Isn't everything we do?

'Yes, but this would not just cause punishments. It could cost
the lives of those willing to help us.'

We all understood that when we agreed to help, she writes.

The thought is foreign to me. Death did not cross my mind

when I took this endeavor on. I'm going to die anyway. 'Did you, really?'

We did.

Well then, there's nothing to hold us back. Nothing except my own fears and worries. 'What if we poisoned the Grand Chancellor's food?'

She's silent.

Though I haven't seen him eat, he's always taken a small tray of food in the evenings and it comes back empty. There has to be a way to get to it. To get to him.

'Like I said, dangerous. But if we can do it, it will be an easy fix. No wars or rebellions that will kill innocent people just trying to earn the right to live. No coming up with another plan to get rid of him. Just a simple dose of poison, and it's all over.'

She rubs her nose before finally writing, *If we didn't get caught at it, it would work.*

The recognition from someone else that the plan has merit makes me feel better, though it's still dangerous. 'That's my biggest concern. Getting caught. We need a good poison. One that's untraceable. Do you know anyone who can help with that?'

Cook would know.

Of course. I should have thought of him myself. Especially after the kindness he's shown me, and not just with the tea. Now I think about it, he's always been kind. This doesn't mean he'll help kill the Grand Chancellor. 'Do you think he'd be willing?'

More than willing. He'll wonder why he didn't come up with the idea himself.

'How do you know that?'

I haven't lived here this long without discovering at least a few others unhappy with the Grand Chancellor's rule.

I suppose she has, dangerous as it sounds. 'Now the trick is writing the idea to him without getting caught in the process. And if we go forward with it, acquiring the poison.'

I have time alone with him in the kitchens very early in the morning. Then would be a good time, I think.

'I will leave it in your hands then.' Which makes me even more nervous than taking it on myself. If she gets caught in the process of getting the message to him, it will mean both their lives. I'd rather it be me taking that risk. Though if they get caught, they'll be questioned as well. There's no telling if they'll be able to keep my involvement out of this, or not tell on the other tarnished who are unhappy here. I'll just have to trust that all will go well.

I gather up the slips of paper and burn them so there's no evidence left. Then I instruct Three to make certain she destroys all evidence of her talk with cook or bring it to me. It's going to be nerve-wracking until this is all over.

* * *

I sit on the couch while Nathaniel plays with Abby. She's grown too big, and I've grown too scared. Knowing Nathaniel wants his father out of power is much different than telling him I've helped with a plot to get rid of the Grand Chancellor for good. I hope he's not too angry with me and that the plan works. The question is, how do I tell him?

'You're supposed to be sleeping,' Nathaniel spells to me.

I can do this. I can. 'There's something I need to say.'

He brings the baby over and sits next to me. 'What is it?'

'It's not easy to.'

'Are you well? Is something bad going to happen to you?'

'Only if you're too upset at what I've done.'

'Now you're scaring me,' he spells. 'What's happened?'

I take a deep breath and let it out, nice and slow. 'I've helped with a plan to have the Grand Chancellor...'

'What is it? You can tell me.'

'To have him poisoned.' There. I said it.

'That's what you're so worried about? That I'll be upset over it?'

'Yes.'

'Bethany, I would do the job myself if I could.'

He doesn't know how much of a relief that is to read.

'My father comes in here every Sunday to try and gauge my mood.' he spells out to me.

'Interesting. That's the most human I've ever heard of him being.'

He shrugs. 'I'm apathetic to it all. I try not to lie, but I can't bring myself to go along with him, either. He wants so desperately for me to start training to take his place. I'm afraid if Nelly is able to give him a son, he'll have me killed.'

Fathers. Why would they treat their children this way? After talking with Waverly throughout the time I've known her, I know this isn't a common practice in Envado. Why does it have to be so here? Why can't they treat us with love and cherish us? I'm afraid the answer will never be known. Not only that, but at least my father and Nathaniel's won't be changing anytime soon, if ever.

CHAPTER 32

I leave a note for Serena, telling her we have a plan in the works —without going into detail, in case it's found—and make my way to the kitchen. If Cook is going to risk his life to make this happen, I want to make certain he knows how grateful I am, even if I can't say it.

On my way there, I cross paths with another tarnished. I expect her to just walk by, but instead she reaches out to me as we come near each other. She grabs hold of my arm and gives it a squeeze. When I look up, she adds a small smile.

She's gone quickly after, and I can't help but wonder what this was about. I don't even know the particular tarnished, which isn't unusual. There are many tarnished here I still don't know. But why then would she stop me like that?

As soon as I reach the kitchen, Cook greets me with a big smile. "Wondering when I would see you and little Ben again."

"And here we are," I reply.

Cook beats me to the ice box and prepares a bottle for Abby. It's strange to think he has such an attachment to my little sister but doesn't even know her real name. Though I suppose I don't know Cook's real name either. I wonder if

Cook would still adore Abby as much if he knew the truth about her gender.

"Can I feed him?" Cook asks as soon as the bottle is ready.

"Of course." I unwrap my makeshift sling and hand Abby over to him, though I won't dare leave the room. Not after all the problems I've had with Nathaniel and Three discovering her gender. People tend to be a little too helpful when it comes to Abby. As much as I appreciate it, now is not the time for accepting that type of generosity. Not if I want to keep her safe.

"You're a natural," I tell Cook. And he certainly is, holding Abby so tenderly while feeding her from the bottle. He looks more in place than I would have guessed. It's too bad tarnished are made barren. I could see Cook making a great dad. Or grandpa, rather, since he looks to be a bit older.

"Thank you. If things were different... But no need for wishful thinking. Not now."

I sit while he finishes feeding the baby. The break is nice, and Cook doesn't make me feel as if I have to speak. It's a nice change. I don't always know what to say to people but feel like I need to say something. At least to those I consider friends. Those I serve as a tarnished I could care less about.

Except for Nathaniel. It's a joy to serve him, though I technically never say anything to him. Our conversations always feel natural and at ease. It's rare to find that in others.

"There we go." Cook puts down the bottle. "Now we just need a good burping."

Several good burps latter, Cook hands Abby back to me. I snuggle her close in my arms, unsure whether or not I'm glad she's with me just this moment.

"I was just about to make some biscuits," he says. "Are you off duty?"

"I am."

"You can sit with me while I make them, then. Unless of course you'd like to go rest."

"Like Ben will let me."

Cook gives me a knowing look. "Babies can be awful hard to get to sleep."

He pulls out the flour, salt, lard, and buttermilk.

"How do you know so much about little ones?" I ask.

"Before I came here, I helped take care of the young ones at a tarnished house for a short time."

Oh. The males who are tarnished because they don't have enough magic. "What age did they come to the house?" Because for all I know about our society and how they treat women, I know little about the men. Only that they are tested at an early age, unlike women who are left to work in the house before being tarnished or sold off.

"They're tested around one year of age. They came to us soon after that, if they had no magic."

I hug Abby closer to me. At least there's some time before they will test her. I have to get her out of here before then. If I can. Really, I only have until the tournament to help her. I have no idea when that will be. It's easy to lose track of time in here, but I do know it's getting closer.

"I can't imagine giving away a child so young."

"Neither can I." He mixes the dough before dusting the table with flour. "Just need to roll these out."

Instead of rolling them out, he writes in the flour dust with his finger. *It's happening tonight.*

I nod my understanding and look around. He's already wiped the flour clear of words for the next thing he writes. When I'm certain there's no one else around, I spell out, 'Thank you. I wish you the best of luck.'

Just hope it works.

'Me, too.' Far more than words can express.

Footsteps near the kitchen. Cook wipes his hand across the flour, ridding it of any remnants of his writing. If only we can do the same to the Grand Chancellor.

CHAPTER 33

I take Abby out of her sling and let her roll around on the floor while I pace the length of the room. There's no way I can handle this tension again. The poisoning had better be successful. If it's not—

No, I can't think that way. It will work. It has to.

I spend the next half hour wearing out the rug while my nerves make a mess of me. When Three comes in the room, I don't need to be told anything. By her pale face and big, scared eyes, I can tell things went badly. Very badly.

"The Grand Chancellor would like to see us all in the ballroom," she says.

Oh, no! This can't be a good sign at all. He's never asked this of us since I've been here.

I'm tempted to run, but there's no way off this property, and hiding will only make things worse. Besides, maybe it's not as bad as I think. Maybe he knows someone tried to poison him, but not who. It could still end all right for us. Maybe.

I wrap Abby back up in her sling and follow Three down to the ballroom. It's already full of tarnished, with more coming in. I didn't know there were this many of us. How many on our side, and how many would rather just follow the Grand Chancellor's rules?

What's more, what if we had all these tarnished and the many others across the country on our side fighting against him during that final battle? Would the outcome have been different? As much as I don't want to think so, I think it would have. We should have embraced them, and we tried, but some people are just so stubborn. They couldn't accept the tarnished. Regardless of the fact that tarnished don't have magic, they are still useful. What is the point of this all, if we can't get freedom for everyone, not just women?

My thoughts spin around this many times, until the room is full of tarnished. The doors slam closed, and the Grand Chancellor appears with father at his side. None of them look pleased to be here. Not that they should. We're to be ignored, not seen or heard or bothered with. Yet here we are, right in the face of them all.

This is worse than I thought it was going to be if he brought into this the only two people left in government besides him.

"A serious crime has been committed today." The Grand Chancellor's voice booms through the room and sends a chill through me. "One of you thought you could get away with trying to poison me. You were wrong."

With a wave of his hand, Cook flies up into the air from the middle of the group. My heart falls to the ground.

"This is the culprit. I want all of you to see what happens when you try to cross me." He snaps his fingers, and a loud, raging scream comes from Cook. It echoes through the room until it makes my ears ache. I press my hands against Abby's ears, hoping to muffle the sound. She starts crying, as do some of the other tarnished. I want to as well, but the tears won't come.

What was father thinking, letting a baby come into a situation like this one? She may not remember it, but that doesn't mean she should be here in the first place.

My heart aches for Cook. I wish I never brought up the idea in the first place. He's so kind and thoughtful. I shouldn't have put him in this situation. This torture is my fault. And what good has come of it? Nothing. Nothing but scaring the tarnished even more.

Finally, the screams stop, cutting off mid-cry. With a flick of his wrist, the Grand Chancellor releases his body, sending it crashing to the ground in the midst of us tarnished. I can't help the cry that comes out of my mouth or the tears that spring to my eyes. There are some lines even the cruelest of people shouldn't cross. The Grand Chancellor just crossed one of them. He's made it more personal than ever.

This hasn't made me want to stop my fight against him. It's only made my need stronger. Not only that, but I've made a decision. Next time there's a chance to take down the Grand Chancellor, I will do it myself.

CHAPTER 34

I think about all the things I want to tell Serena. There's so much. Too much. All my thoughts are a jumbled mess. If I can't make sense of them, how is she going to?

Prioritize them. First, she should know how many tarnished are in this household alone. There must be more than we ever dreamed around the entire country. Who knew it would be so many?

Next, she needs to know the plan failed. Which should be first, really. I just don't want to think about it. We need things to go better than this. No wonder we lost the battle. But I can't think like that. I want to win the war.

Anything else of critical importance? Probably, but I send off the note with just the two most important things. I can't get my thoughts clear enough to make more sense of what she should know.

As soon as the message is off, I make my way to Nathaniel's room to give him his evening meal and clean his room. Or rather, he'll eat and clean while I take a nap. That's what our habit has become. Only tonight, I'm thinking that's not going to happen. I can't stand the image of Cook falling to the floor. I'll have nightmares for years.

Nathaniel is eager to see me, though his face is somber. 'I'm guessing things didn't go well since we're still under lock down.'

'It'd be a correct guess.'

'What happened?'

I go over it with him best I can. It's so exhausting. All I want to do is go back to yesterday, before this weight settled on me. 'It shouldn't have gone like this. I don't even know how your father found out.'

'He always seems to know everything.'

'He doesn't know about us.'

Nathaniel smiles at me. 'No, he certainly doesn't.'

Us. I like the sound of that. Not a *he and I*, but a *we*. Together. I lean into him, and he wraps his arms around me. It's the most natural thing in the world. Until I hear the door open.

I scramble away from him, taking my cleaning supplies with me.

"Nathaniel." The voice that speaks sends chills through me. The *we* that was so special just moments ago almost becomes just a Nathaniel. The Grand Chancellor is the one interrupting. He wouldn't hesitate to kill me if he knew the relationship I'm developing with his son.

Just seeing the Grand Chancellor here makes me want to vomit. As he speaks to Nathaniel, I get busy cleaning the window and hope Nathaniel doesn't mind my eavesdropping into the conversation.

"It's over. You're done."

What? Does that mean the Grand Chancellor discovered what we've been doing? That his son has been spending time with a tarnished, and we're both enjoying it? What type of punishment will Nathaniel come to because of this? And will I be sentenced to a death sooner than at the tournament?

"I don't know what you speak of," Nathaniel counters.

"You know exactly what I'm talking about."

"Why don't you enlighten me?" Nathaniel folds his arms across his chest, holding his head high.

The Grand Chancellor zaps out a brilliant red spell that shoots around the room with vivid deadliness. I duck as it hits just above my head. The movement catches the Grand Chancellor's eye.

"This is what you care about," the Grand Chancellor shouts, motioning to me. "Worthless tarnished, lower class, and women. Do you know they almost killed me?"

"They did?" Nathaniel replies, in what I hope is a voice convincing enough to have his father believe him.

"Yes, they did. Their stupidity and lack of being in our bloodline should prove to you they don't belong anywhere but serving us. But no. You have to insist they have rights. That they are people too. Did their attempt on my life finally change your mind, or are you still on their side?"

"I'm sorry your life was almost taken. But it doesn't mean they are not good people in general. People who deserve better than you give them."

The Grand Chancellor flares his nose, the only warning I get before his arm shoots out toward me. All I see is a flash of crimson, and then I'm on my knees, screaming. The pain is excruciating. The only sense I have left is to fall backward and roll so my back faces him, not my front, where Abby is, though I can hear her crying.

Searing. Pain. Torture.

Won't stop. Legs feel like they're breaking. Back stabs. Everything agonized.

"What are you doing?" Nathaniel yells.

"What I must, to get you to come to my side."

Suddenly the pain stops. I gasp for breath.

"Every day you defy me, another tarnished will be tortured." The Grand Chancellor doesn't even give him a chance to respond.

He whirls around and storms out of the room, slamming the door behind him.

Nathaniel is at my side in an instant. "What can I do?"

I try to say I'm fine, but all that comes out is a groan.

His fingers are at my throat, feeling my pulse. He pulls me onto his lap and checks Abby over, before rocking us both in his lap. He buries his head on my chest next to Abby. "I'm sorry. I'm so, so sorry." His voice is muffled.

If it weren't for his guilt, I could stay like this for a long time, letting his comfort ease my pain. But his pain hurts me almost as much as the Grand Chancellor's torture.

"I'm fine," I croak out.

"The most powerful warlock in existence just tortured you. You're not fine."

"Well, when you put it that way…" I give a great sigh, wishing it was as easy to get rid of my pain as it is my breath. "Is the baby all right?"

He looks Abby over again. She's stopped crying now. My worry for her is as great as the agony I still feel. He says, "Just fine. If you hadn't worked so hard to protect him, it might have been different, but there's no injury to anyone but you."

"And I'll be fine."

"Are you sure?"

"Absolutely." In a week or two. At least nothing is broken.

'Which means you can stop worrying,' I spell out to him.

'If that had just happened to me, would you stop worrying just because I said so?'

'Well, no.'

'Exactly.'

Gah. 'What about you? How are you handling this?'

He shrugs. I give him a look, and he rolls his eyes.

'Fine," he spells. 'It was definitely hard to not only hear what he said, but to see him put you through that. I tried to stop him, but even with the extra magic he forced me to take, I wasn't nearly strong enough.'

'You shouldn't have even tried.' Though as I'm snuggled in his arms, I can't say it doesn't warm my heart. Any part of me that isn't writhing in pain is in awe over how wonderful it feels to be with him. Two emotions so far apart, happening at the same time, is confusing. 'Thank you for trying to be there for me, though.'

'I just wish it was enough.'

'I know.'

'I am sorry his life was almost taken,' Nathaniel suddenly spells to me. 'Sorry it wasn't taken all the way.'

'About that, we couldn't be more in agreement.'

We're both silent for a while, when I ask, 'What are we going to do about his threat?'

'What do you mean *we*? The threat was directed at me.'

'But I'd like to help, if I can.'

'I don't even know what to do about it, let alone how you can help.'

We both sit there in silence, soberness permeating the room.

'How long is it until the tournament?' I ask.

'I'm not sure. It's soon, I think.'

'Do you think you can handle trying to get on your father's good side until then?'

'I don't know if I can do it. Why?'

'Because I have another plan.'

And this one has a greater chance for success. I hope.

CHAPTER 35

'What does this plan entail?' Nathaniel asks.

'It's twofold, and I think one of the parts will have to work,' I spell. 'If he thinks you're on his side, would he let you be with him more?'

'Yes. I used to always be with him.'

'And you said you'd be willing to kill him yourself, yes?'

'Ah.' He sits back in his seat. 'Yes, I'm more than willing, but it's something I've thought of before. I just never thought I could really do it. Until now. I've seen him hurt too many people. I should have tried long ago. Maybe if I had, you wouldn't have been tarnished.'

'Maybe so, but then I wouldn't have all this time to spend with you.'

The heat of a blush spreads throughout my body. He grins up at me, like he knows exactly how I'm feeling.

'What's the second part of your plan?' he spells out.

'You know your father is planning on sacrificing me at the tournament?'

'Unfortunately, I do.'

'Well, if you can get on your father's good side, maybe you can also help me find a way not to have to take califrasum.'

'You want to go to a sacrificial altar without anything to numb you?'

'Only because it means I'll be fully aware when he takes my magic power.'

He smiles, like he understands where I'm going with this. 'And getting drunk on it.'

'Exactly.'

'I like the way you think.' He frowns. 'Except there's too much risk for you still. What if you can't attack him in time? What if he takes too much blood? What if it's all for naught?'

'Then you'll be there at his side, ready to attack him from behind, even as I attack him from the front,' I spell out. 'Besides, do you have a better plan?'

'No. I just wish I could be the one to risk it all.'

'You're still risking a lot, but I know what you mean. I'd rather you not be in danger at all either. But we'll have the perfect opportunity, if you can help me gain it.'

'I'll do my best.'

'I know you will.'

His words of reassurance are better than anything else I could have. Somehow, we *will* make this work.

CHAPTER 36

The next morning is a sad affair at breakfast. There's already a new cook, who is the only one to makes any noise during the meal. Mostly it's just quiet mourning for a man who was trying to do what was right.

As I leave with Three to let Abby stretch, I realize it's time to be more aggressive. Father would do anything to keep his one and only baby boy safe. If he knows what the Grand Chancellor did to me while I had Abby with me, it's sure to be trouble.

'I have an idea,' I spell out to Three as soon as we're alone in the room. 'This time, the risk will be minimal.'

She lifts her shoulders and raises one hand, palm up, as if to say, *what is it?*

'Remember how the Grand Chancellor hexed me?'

She nods.

'How do you think my father would react if he knew the Grand Chancellor did it while I had Ben with me?'

She widens her eyes, mouth open. Then she smiles, as if to say, *let's do this.*

'The only real risk is if my father throws his temper at the gossipers.'

She tilts her head to the side, as if thinking. After a moment, she shrugs and gives me a thumbs up.

'You think we should try?'

She nods. This would be so much easier if we could talk to each other. Sometimes I miss the sound of my own voice. It's going rusty from disuse. I don't get to speak to the other tarnished nearly enough. It's mostly just work, work, work.

'Who are the servants are around my father, then?'

As we hash out the rest of the details, I just have to hope that whatever happens, there's no serious consequences to the gossipers or to Abby. Mostly, I hope the plan works. I hope the Grand Chancellor feels my father's wrath. The wrath I've lived with my entire life.

* * *

AFTER I'M DONE with my work for the day, I go to check on Tawny. I'm lucky if I even see her at all, with all the tarnished in this place; it's difficult to find just one except Three. I don't how I'm possibly supposed to protect Tawny under these conditions. The best I can manage is to check in on her as often as I can.

I find her asleep in a different bedroom than the one I sleep in. I sit on the floor next to her and rest my back against the wall. I bounce the baby, as is a habit now. I often don't even think about the extra weight I carry, not after the scare of being thrown by the Grand Chancellor.

It can't remain this way for much longer. The older she gets, the more she will not just want to get down and play, but need to. Part of me wishes father would just get her a nurse so she would be free to roam, but I know that solution would be the worst for her.

I rest my head back against the wall. Next thing I know, someone is tapping me on the shoulder.

"Good morning, sleepy head," Tawny whispers, probably so as

not to wake the others. "I thought you'd want to go get in your own bed. You look uncomfortable there."

I stand and stretch my worn body. "I am."

We walk out of the room, but instead of going directly to my sleep quarters, I pull her into the room we use for Abby to wiggle around.

'How have you been doing?' I spell out. 'Are you safe? Well?'

She gives me a questioning look. 'As safe as I can be in this place. Exhausted, even though I just got done with my sleep time.'

I'm relieved she seems to be safe, even though there's not a thing I could do about it if she wasn't. 'I know what you mean. It's like they're trying to make us crazy with the lack of sleep.'

'It's working.'

I hesitate a moment and then spell out, 'Is there something I should know about you? The note I got expressed real worry over you, and I can't stop thinking about it.'

She sighs and looks around the room as if someone is going to magically appear.

'It's as safe as it can be to talk in this place.'

She gives a sort of half nod and seems to decide something. 'I am third in line for the throne of Envado.'

I can't help the gasp that comes out of me. 'What in the world are you doing in Chardonia?'

She shrugs. 'I thought I was helping.'

'Helping yourself get in trouble.'

I take a note from Zade's book and begin pacing the room. I'm locked up and tarnished with Envado royalty. No wonder the note said to keep her safe. It's a miracle all of Envado hasn't come marching in for her. I wonder why they haven't. Or maybe they have. Not like I would know, stuck in this house, and the Grand Chancellor is so strong, I don't know if even Envadi are strong enough to defeat him.

'You can't tell anyone,' she spells to me.

'Of course. Your secret's safe with me. I just can't believe you would come here.'

'I wanted to do good.'

This isn't doing anyone any good, but of course I don't tell her that. 'I know how you feel. It's hard to watch things happen you can't do anything about.' Years of watching Serena hexed and tortured on our behalf fly through my memories.

'It must be harder for you. You've lived through it much longer than I have,' Tawny says.

'But I didn't know any different until the last couple of years. You've known all along.'

'Yet I took advantage of my royalty.' She sighs. 'If I ever get free of this place, I'll never take advantage of it again.'

I'd like to reiterate my own feelings on the matter, but I just can't bring myself to. Despite my plans, I fear what may actually happen isn't what should.

CHAPTER 37

A few days later, I'm dusting out the library when another
tarnished servant comes into the room. At first, I pay her
no mind, but then she comes right over to me.

"I'm to take the baby with me," she says.

"What? No, you can't." Panic strums through me.

"By order of Chancellor Stephen, I have to."

"But where are you taking him?" Oh please. This can't be
happening. What have I done?

"He's been ordered to be put under the care of mistress Nelly."

Oh, lands. It could be so much worse I suppose, but still, how
am I to take care of Abby if Nelly has her? I'll have to make certain
Nelly is the only one to look after her except for me. And I'll have
to tell Nelly the truth. The panic in me grows to a thrashing
volcano.

"Can I take him up?" I ask.

"If you're done with your chores here."

Like they could tell if I wasn't. Really, how often does one
bookshelf need to be dusted? "I just finished."

She eyes me like she doesn't believe me. I stay calm on the
outside, even though inside I'm raging. I try to give her the best

example of a servant I can. It's only when she speaks that I know how well I accomplished that feat.

"All right. You can go. I need to work in the gardens anyway," she says. "Straight up to Nelly, mind you. There'll be no dilly dallying."

"Of course." I hurry from the room to both make the point that I won't linger and get out of there before she changes her mind.

The entire way to Nelly's room, my nerves are going crazy. How is she going to react to Abby being a girl? Will she keep the secret for me, or will she tell in order to be in better standing with the Grand Chancellor? I don't think she'll tell. She's been good at trying to help so far, but this is big. How can she ignore it? This secret just keeps getting away from me more and more.

When I finally reach her room and slip inside, my heart is pounding so hard it feels as if someone is hexing it.

Nelly sits on the bed, looking down at Abby and talking softy to her. I ache to take my sister back. I don't trust anyone else with her. No one knows her needs like I do. No one knows how to protect her like I do. Though maybe that's a mistake, since I've done such a poor job at it so far.

"You're here," Nelly says, bringing me out of my morose thoughts. "I wondered how long it would take you."

"I just wanted to know what's going on." I have to choose my words carefully. The Grand Chancellor may be listening. I'll send Nelly a spell, but he's going to need an excuse from me as well. "Had to make sure he's well looked after since he was my charge for so long."

"Of course you do. I may still need your help sometimes anyway. I've never looked after a baby before."

Never looked after a baby? How can she be given the job if she doesn't even know what she's doing? "I am happy to assist in any way I can," I say. 'What happened? Why did they bring him to you?' I spell out, not yet willing to reveal Abby's gender, even though it's inevitable.

'Your father found out about you being hexed,' she spells back. 'He insisted the baby be away from the unsafe tarnished who was liable to be punished.'

Unsafe tarnished? It was the Grand Chancellor who was a fool with my little sister's life, not me. 'So he had the baby brought to you?'

'He said I was the only person in this house capable of taking care of the baby. I don't know why he didn't take it to Nathaniel's mother. She's at least raised a child before. I have yet to do so.'

'He probably didn't think the details through.' I hope that didn't sound too harsh an opinion of her. 'I'm certain you'll do a fine job caring for the baby.'

She beams. I have to trust her. I only hope her extra interactions with the Grand Chancellor don't lead to an accidental discovery that would be catastrophic for Abby.

'There is one thing you need to know,' I spell out.

'What is that?'

'Benjamin is not...' How does one say this?

'Not what?'

Serena would do a much better job than me, spitting out what needs said. 'Benjamin is actually a little girl.'

Nelly widens her eyes, and her mouth falls open. "What?" she asks aloud.

I hurry to cover her mistake. "I would be happy to change his nappy for you, if the job isn't to your liking."

She stares at me a moment like I've suddenly gone mad before she catches on. "Why yes, that would be most helpful."

It's time to change Abby anyway. And then she's going to want a nap. How is Nelly supposed to know any of this? How will she ever care for my sister properly? My father is an idiot for bringing these circumstances upon us when we were getting along so well.

As I move to change Abby's nappy, I give Nelly instructions on how to take care of little Abby. I'm afraid I'm forgetting something, but there's nothing for it. I keep reminding myself that I'm in the same house so I won't be far, but it doesn't make it any easier.

I spell out, 'Please don't say anything. I don't know what they'd do to her if they found out she's a girl.'

'Your secret is safe with me.'

Relief floods through me, but I hold on to my reservations. 'What about the Grand Chancellor? Don't you have to spend a lot of time with him as his wife?'

She shrugs. 'He won't be wanting anything to do with changing nappies; that much I can tell you.'

Thank goodness. "The baby will be tired now. He likes to be rocked to sleep."

"I think that's one thing I can do."

I finish putting on a clean nappy and press Abby close to me. I'm not ready to give her up. I have no choice, though. I hand her over to Nelly, not wanting to let go but somehow managing to. As soon as I do, Abby starts to cry.

Nelly holds her out away from her body, letting my little sister scream instead of comforting her. I clench my teeth, trying to not make the worst of an already bad situation.

"What do I do with he—him?"

I clench my teeth harder at the near slip. That had better be the one and only time she does it, or this isn't going to last. "You need to comfort *him*. Snuggle him in close to you while you rock him."

Nelly does as I directed, and Abby's sobs becoming sleepy whines.

"There you go," I whisper.

"He's never done this before when I've played with him."

"That's because it was never nap time."

"I think I'm going to need you even more than I thought."

I hold back a smile. If I can't be with my sister all the time, at least I'm still needed. What's more, she's somewhere safe and close by. It's not enough, though. I've got to find a way to get her out of here, before things get rough.

CHAPTER 38

As soon as I walk in the room, Nathaniel zips a spell to me. 'Where's Abby?'

Not where she's supposed to be. I let out a heavy sigh. 'Stephen heard about what happened with your father and decided I wasn't a suitable caregiver on my own. Nelly has her.'

It's the first time I've referred to my father as *Stephen*, but after everything, it feels more fitting than *father* does. If he doesn't want to acknowledge me as his daughter, I don't have to acknowledge him as my father.

I set Nathaniel's food tray at his table, wishing against all wishes I brought different news.

Nathaniel jumps up beside me and takes hold of my hand. 'Is Nelly trustworthy?'

'Yes. I'm more worried about your dad being around Abby than about Nelly. She says he won't bother the baby at all, but accidents happen. He could come in the room at the wrong time, and it'd all be over.'

Nathaniel wraps me in a hug. I lean into him like I always want to do. The hurt and worry inside me jumble together in a mass that even his comfort is hard pressed to sooth. Despite that, I still hold on as tight as I can, not wanting to ever let go.

Of course, we can't stay like this forever. Not in this house. When we let go of each other, he spells, 'I'm so sorry.'

'It's your father's and mine's fault.' I sigh again. 'Well, and my fault. I told Three we should let it slip to Stephen what happened with your father while I had Abby with me. Stephen seems to be the only one left who might have a chance at bringing him down, and I thought there would be consequences against your father. Instead, Abby got taken away.'

He puts an arm around me, making my shuddering breath calm.

'I've already sent a note to Serena,' I continue to spell out. 'We're going to try to get Abby out of here. I think she'll be easier to sneak out than a fully grown person. And Nelly is going to start spreading the task of watching her to several different tarnished, me included. I'll still have access to her and her room. I'm thinking of sneaking Abby out while Nelly is asleep, so even she doesn't know who did it.'

'That's dangerous for both you and Nelly.'

'But even more dangerous for Abby to stay. Think how many people know her secret now. And their number continues to grow. We have to get her out before my father discovers it.'

'Let me help, at least,' he says.

'I don't mean to be unkind, but how? You're stuck in here.'

'Yes, but I still have connections. I hope they are enough.'

'What are you thinking, then?'

'Katherine. She's the tarnished you introduced me to. If she can come here without going the formal route, she'll be able to leave with Abby.'

'That might work. There are tarnished who come and go, delivering food. I could send a message to Serena and get it all set up,' I spell.

'The tricky part may be getting her away from Nelly without her realizing it's you doing so.'

I shrug. 'What does it matter? I'm to be sacrificed soon enough, anyway. What difference does it make if I get in more trouble before then?'

He takes a hold of my hand, looking me straight in the eye. 'I don't want them to hurt you—to torture you because they catch you in the act. And they aren't going to sacrifice you if there's anything I can do about it.'

A flutter moves through me at his words, but I can't let it deter me. Besides, as nice as the thought is, as things stand right now, there's nothing he can do to save me. 'I don't want it either, but it's better than letting my sister stay here.'

He squeezes my hand and pulls me closer. 'Please promise you'll at least try to figure out a way that won't get you in trouble unless necessary.'

With the way he makes my heart pound, I would promise just about anything to him. I say, 'I'll try, but you know I only have so much control over it.'

He pulls away and brushes a hand through his hair. 'Don't I know it? But as long as you do your best...'

'I will.'

'That will have to be enough.'

There's a moment of silence as we both absorb what I'm going to try. I can't let it last. Not when there's still so much to do.

'Now that I'm not the full caregiver to Abby, I think there's something I should do.'

'From the look in your eye, I'm not going to like the sound of it.'

I shrug one shoulder. 'Well... it's about Zade.'

'Knew it.'

'Let's just think about it for a moment. I don't have Abby, and you're trying to get on your father's good side.'

'That's true,' he spells, 'but I don't see how that would make a difference about you seeing Zade.'

'What if you gave me a note that was for Zade? Something about how you're glad your father is'—I swallow—'doing away with him at the tournament. But really, I'll be letting him know Serena and my siblings are well.'

And helping him, if there's anything I can do. While Nathaniel mulls the plan over, I think about all the things Zade's missed. He doesn't even know mother had twins and one was a boy. Or that we tried to free him. Though perhaps it's good he doesn't know how bad things got.

'I don't like it, but it is a good idea,' Nathaniel spells.

I smile.

'If I tell you where to go,' he spells, 'I want you to be careful.'

'I will be.'

He gives me directions on how to get there and then writes a note about how Zade was part of the reason his life was ruined, and Nathaniel hates him for it. Not true, but a good enough reason for the guards. It was partly Zade's fight that got Nathaniel here in the first place. If Zade never came to Chardonia, things would be so much different.

'What do you think?' he asks.

'It's sufficiently rude. Zade would be hurt if I weren't the one delivering the note. I think if your father finds out, he'll be pleased with you.'

'There's no if about it. He will find out. Sometimes I wonder how we've gotten away with being together so long, without him finding out about us.'

I lean into him. 'I'm so grateful he hasn't.'

He pulls me in closer, and I tilt my head toward him. As soon as our lips meet, fire burns through me. I wrap my arms around him. Never have I felt the way I do about him. He makes my heart soar, even when it should be failing.

I kiss him back again and again, loving the way we fit together.

We should have done this a long time ago. This perfect mixture of romance and passion, all bundled up in one kiss that I never want to end.

Together we're like one. One heart. One mind. One soul.

All I want is to keep this feeling. To keep us together, no longer separated by circumstances. To be free of this society and his father.

But right here and now that freedom seems to matter less and less. I want to be with him forever. To turn this friendship we have into something more. Much more. And judging by the feeling behind his lips on mine, he wants something much more as well.

I'm reluctant to end the kiss, but it can't go on, especially in this house. When it does finally end, I pull him back for another peck on the mouth.

'There's one nice thing about Abby not being here,' I spell.

'What's that?'

'It's good to be close to you.'

'And I think it's wonderful to be close to you.' He pulls me even closer, hugging me to him.

I smile up at him, wishing moments like this were what life was about. But it can't be. There's too much danger. Too many people fighting against us. One who matters the most—and that's the person closest to him besides me. No matter how much I enjoy my time with Nathaniel, the Grand Chancellor is always there, waiting to pounce.

CHAPTER 39

The first thing I take care of is Abby. All we have to do is get her off the Grand Chancellor's grounds, and Cynthia will be waiting for her. That's all. The thought makes me want to give an insane laugh. If the task was that easy, I would have done it long ago. Hopefully, for her, it will be.

Plan. I'll check to make certain Nelly is sleeping. She should be this time of night, but if not, I'll say I came to see if she wanted some company. If she is, I'll sneak the baby out. Then I'll pass the baby to Three, who will take her to the delivery man Nathaniel sent a note to through the same chain. The delivery guy should have Katherine with him, and together they will hide Abby with his goods and take her off the grounds. And hopefully to Cynthia.

I only hope everything goes smoothly and that the rocking of the cart is enough to keep Abby from crying. And that no one's looking for a baby escaping on the cart, just a tarnished, who's much bigger. That's a lot of hoping.

I finish my chores for the day and head toward Nelly's room. It's a long way there, as is to anywhere in this house. Usually I'm accustomed to it, but today it feels tense. Like each step is another toward some unknown danger, not to gaining Abby's freedom.

Nelly meets me at the door. Her face is drawn, but her words are cheerful. "It's the most wonderful thing. You'll be so happy to hear the news."

"What news is that?" I'm disappointed she's awake, so we can't go forward with the plan today. How hard is it going to be for Cynthia and Lukas to hide out another day? For Katherine to come back again? They had better stay safe.

"It's about Benjamin," she says, yanking my little fears into great big ones.

"What about him?"

"Stephen married again last night, and his new wife is going to be taking care of Benjamin now."

My heart sinks all the way to the floor and beyond. How could this have happened when we were so close to getting her out? Why now?

"Has he gone with her yet, or do you still have him?"

"He's already gone," she says, and then mouths, "I'm so sorry."

How could this be? What is my father's new wife going to do once she realizes the baby boy she's to be taking care of is a girl? I stumble away from Nelly, not hearing whatever else she says to me.

Stephen remarried? My father? He can't have. He just can't. What are we going to do? Her secret is certain to get out now.

'I'm sorry,' Nelly suddenly spells out. I brush the words away, unable to take her pity, but she persists. 'It's my fault she's gone.'

That gets my attention. All one-hundred percent of it on her. 'What do you mean, your fault?'

She bites her lip, not saying or spelling anything.

I round on her, moving closer, my heart pumping hard. 'What do you mean, Nelly?'

'I know you were trying to get Abby out of the house, and I didn't want her to go. I've come to love her so much.'

A feeling of panic comes over me. I've never felt such strong anger. For the first time in my life, I get the smallest glimpse at why Stephen must have beat and hexed us all those years. I can't be like him, and yet this anger roiling through me demands some sort of release. I need to channel it into doing some good.

'What did you do?' I spell.

'I told the Grand Chancellor I thought there was a plot to get her out of the house. But don't worry. I didn't name you.'

'You didn't name me?' I want to scream. Instead, my spelled words grow bigger and deep, deep red in color. 'Didn't name me? Do you realize what you've done? Abby is going to be found out, and then what will happen to her? What will happen to me, for taking care of her so long and not saying something? What will happen to you?'

Her face goes pale. 'I didn't know he would respond like this. I didn't know. I thought he would give me guards or something.'

'We have to get her out of here. Today. Now. This very instant.'

'But I can't.'

'Why not?' I demand.

She looks down, her message spelled to me in small letters made of yellow and green. 'I'm scared.'

I want to rage against her. To scream and yell.

But I don't.

I give her a stern look. 'You made this mess. You will help me fix it. I can't go get my sister—not now—so you will go get her for me.'

She shakes her head.

'You will,' I spell out in big, bold letters. 'You have to, for Abby's sake.'

'For Abby.' She presses her eyes closed tight. 'What do I do?'

CHAPTER 40

I wait for Nelly by the servant's entrance. It's a little too close to the hidden-note spot for my comfort. I don't want anyone to get any ideas about searching the place.

Katherine is close by, waiting next to the wagon with the driver. They won't be able to wait much longer without suspicion. The wagon is already unloaded and ready to set out. What is taking Nelly so long?

Last time I saw Katherine, she was growing her hair out. Now it's shaved off again. It was a surprise to learn she chose to fake being a tarnished, though I suppose we all have our reasons for doing things.

After being tarnished for real, I can't imagine wanting to fake it. But then, we've had different life circumstances. I wish I could speak with her about everything that's taken place. Have some comfort in hearing from another person my family is well. But I don't dare say anything. The Grand Chancellor can probably hear even outside, despite there being no walls. He seems to know everything. Or almost everything. I can't be the one to give him even more.

Still, it's hard waiting like this and having her so close but not being able to do or say anything.

Finally, Nelly comes sliding out the servants' entrance, a large basket in hand. A basket I can only hope contains my sister. She hands it to me, and by the weight, I know it has to have little Abby in it. I pull the blanket back, my throat clogging with emotion.

As much as I want this moment to happen, I will miss her dearly. This is no place for a baby, though. Especially a female baby. I rub my finger against her sleeping cheek and cover her back up, making sure to leave enough space for her to breath.

I place the basket in the wagon, my eyes burning. I blink back the tears. They'll have to wait until later to manifest themselves.

An idea hits me then. Nelly is standing there, fingers twisting in on themselves. She helped save my sister. Now I'm going to help save her.

"Go," I say.

Nelly gives me a look, like she doesn't understand what I mean. I don't dare say more, and I can't spell anything out here. I grab her arm and point to the wagon. Her eyes go wide. I point to the wagon with more force. She shakes her head at me.

I glance around. Just the driver that I can see. That doesn't mean there isn't someone else out here, though. It's worth the risk. I move to the wagon and spell on the bed, where it will be harder to see, 'You have to go now. This is your one chance to get free.'

She shakes her head again.

'What? Do you have a spell on you, keeping you here, like the tarnished do?'

She shakes her head.

I'm getting awfully tired of that response, and there's not time to delay. 'Then get in. You're not going to have another chance like this.'

She holds out her hand toward me. At first, I don't know why she would do such a thing, until I realize how bad she's shaking.

'I know you're scared,' I spell. 'You can do this, despite how scared you are. You rescued the baby. Now it's time to rescue yourself.'

At least I hope she rescued Abby. Every moment we delay like this is another moment we may be caught. I only wish I could go with them, but with the spell on the property, to kill me the instant I leave, there's no chance of it happening.

She bites her lip. I grab her shaking hand and guide her to the wagon. To my relief, she lets me help her up into the back. 'Lie down,' I spell.

She lies down next to Abby. I hope Cynthia and Lukas can sneak out one more person. Katherine gives me a nod. I wish there was more we could say to each other, but this isn't the time or place. All I can do is nod back.

With that, the cart is off. I want to watch it go, but I can't draw more attention to it. I brush a tear from my eye and turn around to head back to the house. That's it, then. My sister I've taken care of for so long is gone. I hope she's safe.

CHAPTER 41

"We're all to go to the ballroom," Three says.

"Again?" Fear pounds through me. The others may not know what this is about, but I do. Will the Grand Chancellor be able to tell? Will he know I helped Abby and Nelly escape?

"Again." Her face is grim, probably at the memory of the last time we were there. It was a horrible day. One I don't wish repeated for anyone.

As I make my way to the ballroom, my legs feel wobbly, barely able to hold me up. I don't know how long I'll be able to stand without falling to the ground or passing out. Maybe it would be preferable, but I wonder how much it would give me away. I have to stay strong.

I take several steadying breaths and continue on. I'm in the middle of the ballroom before I know it. People in front of me, and more people crowding in behind me. The entire ballroom quickly fills up. When the Grand Chancellor demands something, it sure doesn't take long to happen.

The Grand Chancellor steps onto the area above us, looking out over the crowd. My legs are weak again, trembling, but I keep them standing strong.

"This household seems to be growing discontent as of late," the Grand Chancellor says. "Something I will not stand for. Who among you knows where the baby and my wife are?"

It's as I feared then. He knows they're missing and is going to make us pay for it.

When no one steps forward, his face grows more intense, if that's even possible. "No one?"

The crowd stays silent. My hands shake like Nelly's did before she left. I keep them fisted at my sides.

"I'll ask one more time. Where is the baby and my wife?"

Still, nobody steps forward. The only one who could is me. Well, and his son, but Nathaniel isn't here. Thankfully. I would hate for him to have to go through this too. His father is much too harsh with him as it is. He doesn't need to add any more crimes to Nathaniel's list.

"Fine. If no one will come forward, you'll all be punished."

Fear stabs at me. Am I really going to make all these people suffer because I'm unwilling to tell? The answer comes back to me. Unfortunately, yes. I can't risk the Grand Chancellor knowing what happened to Nelly and Abby. Not while they may still be in the county. Not when he can still track them down and bring them back. I can't allow it.

I silently apologize to all the tarnished present. I wish there was a way for me to change things, but I don't dare.

Next thing I know, there's a flash of crimson spell, and my back arches outward. I scream, my voice lost in the screams of all those around me. The pain is immense. My entire body swims in agony. It seems to go on forever and ever. Pain and more pain.

When it stops, I collapse to the ground. I gasp for breath, my body numb. I come to realize I'm half on top of someone's legs. Others are on the ground all around me. They didn't deserve this. I expected it for myself even if I didn't deserve it either, but these people are innocent, and because of me, they were just subjected to the most painful kind of torture.

"Now, I hope you understand the serious nature of your crime. Whoever of you knows, it's time to come forth," the Grand Chancellor says.

I cringe. Does this mean we're about to be subjected to even more torture? I can't handle it. For myself, I will bite down on the pain and accept it, but all these other innocents... How can I sit by and let them be tortured because of me? I can't. I just can't do it.

I open my mouth to come forth. Instead of words, another scream unleashes, loud and crude. I writhe in agony. Greater than I've ever felt before. My mind goes numb. Pain.

Pain.

Pain.

When it finally stops, my body feels as if it's continuing anyway, echoes of the ghost of madness coming to me.

The world blurs before me. My body is limp. Someone is lying on my arm, and another someone on my legs. I can't bring myself to care, though. Not when I'm finally free of the torture.

"Since everyone refuses to tell, you will all be docked three hours of sleep for the rest of your time here, and there will be hexes daily." With that, the Grand Chancellor leaves his elevated position to somewhere out of sight.

Still, I don't move. I don't do anything. My eyes burn with tears. Around me there's the sound of crying. I brought this upon us all.

CHAPTER 42

The next day, I'm sore. More than my body hurts, though. My soul is agonized. Guilt floods me over causing every tarnished in this place torture, and not just temporarily. They are going to be short on sleep as well. I never realized the cost of getting Abby away from here would be so high. But then, if I had to do it again, I would. Anything to protect my little sister.

I have to keep living my life the best I can, and that means going through with the next part of my plan. I only hate to think what will happen if the Grand Chancellor realizes his son and I are playing him the fool.

As I make my way to the dungeon with the note gripped tightly in my hand, my palms grow sweaty. I'm going to have the note ruined before I get there, at this rate. It sounded so much easier when I talked to Nathaniel about it. Part of me wants to turn back, but I press forward anyway, unwilling to make Zade wonder what's going on any longer than he already has.

Two guards are standing before the door of the dungeon, just as Nathaniel said there would be. The only two guards in the place. Everything else is guarded by spells directed at every individual imprisoned there.

"What are you doing here?" one of the guards demands.

Just being at the opening of the dungeon makes my knees quiver, but I want to do this. I need to do this. If I wasn't playing a cowering tarnished, I'd pull myself up to my full height. Instead, I let strength fill me and keep my shoulders rounded.

"I was told by Master Nathaniel to bring the prisoner Zade this note." I hold it out for them to see.

"Do you know what it says?"

"No, sir."

He rips it from my hand, reads it, and laughs. "John, read this."

The other guard reads it and laughs as well. "This is just the sort of torture he needs for the day. Go on and take it to him."

For the day? Just how often and how badly do they torture him? They move aside and open the door. I hurry in it, and then turn. "Wait, where is he?"

They laugh and slam the door closed behind me. Just grand. Thank goodness Nathaniel told me where Zade is, or at least where he was, last time Nathaniel came for a visit. But that was some time ago. I'll find him, though. Whatever it takes. I'm more worried about the guards not letting me out of the dungeon.

There's an eerie faint green glow down here, lighting the stairs and covering pretty much everything. My only guess is I'm walking through one of those spells that is tuned into the prisoners. Just thinking about it makes me shiver. If circumstances were different, this spell could be torturing or even killing me, and here I am walking through it.

I follow Nathaniel's directions, keeping in mind the map and how I relate to the exit. Whatever I do, I don't want to lose my way. Just like Nathaniel showed, there are halls, leading off everywhere. This place quickly turns to a maze. No wonder the guards laughed. They think they'll never see me again, or that it'll be a long time if they do. No matter. It will just give me longer to talk to Zade.

The dungeon is cold. Not just physically, but mentally. The

place is dark, with critters I can't see, scurrying about. Stuff's growing on the walls and coming down from the ceiling. It smells rotten, like something died long ago. Knowing the Grand Chancellor, something probably did. Something wet drips on me, and I have to stop myself from calling out. No telling what it could be. There's scratching every so often and a faint whistling howl.

As much as the Grand Chancellor belongs in a place like this, I can't see him coming down here with how crazed he is about keeping everything clean.

It gives me hope that Zade isn't in as bad of a condition as I expected. Not that I know exactly what to expect. Just something horrifying. Of course, even if the Grand Chancellor doesn't come here, it doesn't mean he can't tell his guards to torture Zade. I shiver.

The halls branch off, and it takes more and more willpower to keep going. The place grows darker and stinks of sewage.

I'm almost there, though. I can make it. I can do this for someone who's practically a brother to me. Something brushes against my leg. I let out a squeal. It's probably a good thing I can't see what it is. How can they leave people in a place like this?

I round the last bend and come to a room. At first I see nothing at all—it's so dark—but then I realize part of the wall looks different than the rest.

Zade.

He's thin. Bone thin, in a way that brings tears to my eyes. His hands are stuck in some sort of spelled manacles, the chains giving him some leeway, but not enough. He doesn't look up. Is he... Could he be... dead?

I swallow past my fears and step through the many spells between me and him. What have they done to Zade? He doesn't stir. The Grand Chancellor isn't going to have anyone to sacrifice beside me. As I get closer, I realize his arms and what I can see of his chest are covered in bruises.

I almost don't dare reach out to him, too afraid nothing but a cold, dead body awaits me instead of the Zade I've come to love like a brother. But I can't leave here without knowing for certain if he's gone. I reach out, slowly moving toward him. Suddenly, his hand jumps out and grabs my wrist. I cry out as he yanks me toward him.

"What do you want?" His voice is strong, despite the weakness of his body.

My heart races from fright, but also with relief that he's alive. Serena will be comforted. Though I don't think I can bring myself to tell her how haggard he is. "I have a note for you from the Grand Chancellor's son, Nathaniel."

He laughs, a bitter sound that chills me to the soul, though his eyes have a hint of eagerness for news. "Nathaniel? What could he possibly say to me?"

My hand shakes as I hold out the note. He yanks it from my hand. I don't even wait for him to finish reading it. I spell out, 'It's me, Bethany. I came to check on you.'

His face instantly transforms from a hard, stony thing to one of hurt dismay. He shakes his head.

'Yes, it's me. I was caught trying to escape, and the Grand Chancellor tarnished me. Don't worry, Serena and the rest of my family are safe.'

He closes his eyes and lets out one long, ragged breath.

After some time of silence, I spell out, 'Nathaniel is helping me out. Can you message me back?'

He shakes his hands and points to the spelled manacles around his hands.

Just grand. We have to have a whole conversation, but one sided. I try to think of what else he could want to know. 'We tried to not just rescue you, but to defeat the Grand Chancellor. Waverly brought it all on. You would have been scared for her, but she was very brave.' Tears spring to my eyes as I think about how she was so determined to save him. 'She is desperate to know how you're doing.'

He stands, the chains forcing him keep his arms to the side. He pulls his shoulders back, making himself look better than he really is. It makes me want to let loose my tears, but I blink them away before he can notice.

'I'll make certain both Waverly and Serena know you're alive and...' Not well. He's clearly not well at all, and I can't lie. But he is trying so hard to look like he can do this, I have to say something. 'And brave.'

He nods, like that's what he was hoping for. When he doesn't sit back down, I say, 'Please make yourself as comfortable as you can.'

He opens his mouth as if he wants to protest, but then he closes it and complies.

'Are you hungry? I brought some sausage and bread.'

His eyes grow big as he nods. I hurry to give it to him, so he can eat while we finish talking. 'Do you know if Daniel is close by?'

He shakes his head to the right.

'I'll go to him before I leave as well.'

Zade shovels the food in faster than I've ever seen anyone eat. I should have brought more. Still, I save some for Daniel, as I know Zade would want.

'I'll pass on that message to Serena and Waverly. I'm certain they'll let your parents know. I'll try to come back if it's safe," I spell, and then say, "Did you have a message you want to send back to Nathaniel?"

Finally, he gives a bit of a smile. "Tell him, he's scum."

I grin. Nathaniel will love that reply.

I hurry from the room, not because I want to be away from Zade, but because I still have chores to do before I can get some sleep. Daniel's prison cell is right next door. The hall there doesn't seem quite as dark now that I've found Zade.

After taking care of Daniel and assuring him I'll let Annabelle know where he is, I make my way back out of the maze. It seems as if I've been down here for hours, lost in a world of hopelessness and hexes. No wonder our plan failed so miserably. If this dungeon is enough to hold warlocks and have plenty of spells left over, the Grand Chancellor should be weak with the effort. Or at least have the power spread out between his law officers. Instead, they all seem stronger than normal. Especially the Grand Chancellor. There is no chance we could ever defeat him.

CHAPTER 43

I take a long time to send notes to Waverly and Serena. I don't want to give them false hope, but I also don't want to tell them how bad things are. In the end, I settle for telling them I saw Zade and Daniel and that they are alive. That they miss their loved ones and are hanging in there. It doesn't seem nearly enough.

It doesn't matter, though. The tournament is closer every day. They'll figure out for themselves soon enough just how bad things really are. For now, I want to give them some hope and comfort. They need that.

I need that too, but here, there's nowhere to get it. Everyone is subdued since the torture. At first, I thought they were meek as well as scared, but I notice a fire in several of their eyes. If the Grand Chancellor thinks he beat us down, he's sorely mistaken.

I've been thinking. Maybe poison was too obvious. Maybe the Grand Chancellor found out because he expects things like that to threaten his life. What we need is something he won't expect. Something like an explosion in his own home.

The problem is I don't know how to cause an explosion. What's more, I don't know how to not get caught. If the Grand Chancellor was able to tell Cook was the one who poisoned him, who's to say he wouldn't know I was the one who set off an explosion?

If it works, I won't need to worry about it. If it doesn't work, who knows what will happen?

What I need to do is talk to Nathaniel. He may have some ideas about how to do this. When I go to his room that night, I ask him exactly that.

'Are you out of your mind?' he spells, words flashing with red sparks. 'One person has already been killed, you're going to lose more sleep over it, and more tarnished will be hexed. Do you think an explosion is the way to go?'

'I want to do something. I can't sit by and watch my death draw nearer.'

'I know.' His words glow softer, a pale green. 'It's just that I don't want to see you hurt. Which is why I'm going to work on getting closer to my father.'

'But what if that doesn't work? We need another plan.'

He runs his fingers through his hair. 'Maybe you're right.'

'You'll help me?' Excitement tingles through me.

'I said *maybe*.'

'Why only maybe?' I spell out, confused.

He lets out a huff of air. 'Because I want to help you not be sacrificed. I want to save you. But I fear doing what you suggest will only put you in more danger.'

His words glow bright and make me sit down on a chair. Is he right? Will this put me in more danger? Or will it help me not be sacrificed?

'I think it will help,' I spell out. 'We can figure out something so I don't have to be sacrificed in the first place.'

'But what if we don't? What if it doesn't work and he does nothing but torture you until the sacrifice? I don't know if I could handle it.'

I go to him and take his hand in mine. 'It's worth the risk. Maybe it won't work out, but don't you think we ought to try?'

He doesn't reply for so long, I fear he's never going to. 'I don't want to lose you. I wish I could think of a way to get you out of the sacrifice without putting you in more danger,' he spells out.

'Someone has to do it. It may as well be me.'

He grabs on to me then, pulls me close, and holds me tight. I grab onto him, holding him back. I never want to let go. I never want to have to be brave. But if I'm not, who will be?

CHAPTER 44

'So do you have any ideas how I can do this?' I spell out to
Nathaniel.

'I don't know for certain. Not yet.' He sighs, letting me have
some breathing space again. Not that I want it.

'What about a spell?'

'Knowing my father, he'd find a way to track it.'

'Is there anything he can't track?' I spell.

He shrugs. 'As far as I know, very few things. He didn't know I
was helping you before with the war. He doesn't know we talk. At
least as far as I know.'

I glance around the room, like it's suddenly going to show a
spell the Grand Chancellor cast, but nothing happens. The only
spells around here are the ones we use to talk and the one the
Grand Chancellor put over Nathaniel's door to keep him imprisoned here. Of course we can't know if he's listening to us right
now with a hidden spell.

'We need to find a way to start an explosion without a spell?' I
cast to him.

'Exactly. Even then, we need to be careful.'

'How do we make an explosion without a spell?'

We're both silent with our spells as we think. What can we blow up? I know very little about things like that. Really, I know little at all because of how I grew up. I was trying to learn more before the war, when I had more freedom, but there was little time to learn much of anything. Mostly just a few spells here and there that Waverly or Cynthia had time to teach me. Nothing like how to blow up part of a house.

The house.

'We have to warn the people working in that area of the house,' I spell out the exact same time he casts, 'Grenade.'

'Grenade?' I want to know where he's going before I explain myself. 'Will that work?'

He grins at me, all excited. 'I think it would.'

'I think maybe we can get some through Sanos. If they manage to deliver it safely here.'

'I hope they can. I don't know another way to make an explosion without a spell. I don't know enough about chemistry to do anything more.' After I read that message, he lets it dissolve and puts up, 'What were you saying about warning people?'

'I think we have to, or else innocents will get hurt.'

'We definitely don't want that. How about we get the supplies together and plan when to do it, then warn everyone before it happens?'

'Sounds like a plan.' I bite my lip, hesitating to say more, but this is Nathaniel. If I can't say more to him, there's no one I can talk to. 'I'm scared.'

'The truth is'—he takes a deep breath—'I am too.'

CHAPTER 45

S anos and my sisters deliver. Or maybe it was Waverly. I'm not sure who, but someone got me two grenades. Problem is this means I have to use them. I'm not sure about it; the thought of throwing one makes me uneasy. So I hide them in my skirts and head to Nathaniel's room. It's time to take him dinner, anyway.

I pick up his plate of food and continue on my way. It feels like every servant I pass looks at me like they know I've done something wrong. That's when I see Fredrick.

I try to hurry past him, but he plants his arm out on the wall, stopping me. "What have we here?"

I keep my head down. "I'm just taking the Grand Chancellor's son his dinner."

"Hm." He doesn't move, but he doesn't say anything else either.

What does he expect? Am I supposed to give myself away? Does he know about the grenades in my skirts but wants to hear me confess? It doesn't matter. I'm not doing it. It doesn't stop my hands from sweating, though. If they get any worse, I may just drop Nathaniel's tray.

"Looks like we have trouble here," he says.

My breathing comes in shallow gasps. "No trouble at all."

"Don't mouth off to me. I can see a lot of trouble."

I press my lips together tight, waiting for him to point out the grenades.

"I think this will end up in a hex."

A hex? Is that all? Or is that just the beginning? Maybe it's worse than the hexes I'm accustomed to. Much, much worse.

A bright green spell flashes to me and wraps around both my wrists, burning them. I cry out but don't drop the tray, as much as I want to. I have a feeling things would be even worse if I did.

"Is this enough to pry open your lips to your mistake, or do I need to make things even worse for you?"

My mistake is growing heavy in its hiding place and my mind. Why did I ever think I'd be able to get away with this?

"I can see you're a hard learner. Unfortunately, I don't have time to punish you properly. Another of your faults, holding me up."

I clench my teeth and continue to look down.

"Get your cleaning supplies and go to Nathaniel's room."

My cleaning supplies—that's what I forgot. It's hard not to show how relieved I am. I keep my fingers tight around the tray, my wrists still aching and my teeth clenched. He didn't realize I'm carrying something deadly. In my haste, I forgot something important to him. Nathaniel and I probably won't even use the cleaning supplies tonight.

I hurry away from him, glad he needs to be somewhere. How much worse would it have been if he weren't in a hurry? I'm glad I don't have to find out.

After quickly grabbing the cleaning supplies too, I hurry to Nathaniel's room. Thankfully, this time there's no scary encounter, though the grenades feel as if they might burn a hole against my skin.

The moment I close Nathaniel's door behind me, he spells, 'What happened? You're as white as a sheet."

I set down the cleaning supplies, and he takes the dinner tray from my shaking hands. 'I almost got caught.'

'Doing what?'

I fish the grenades out and show him.

'You got them.' He takes them from me and gently sets them by his tray of food. 'I didn't think we'd actually be able to get our hands on anything that would work.'

'We did, all right. Now, I don't know what to do with them. I thought Fredrick was going to catch me bringing them here.'

'You ran into Fredrick on the way up?'

I nod.

He grabs my hand and with his other one spells out, 'That's bad luck.'

I nod again, my hand shaking inside of his, though I feel a lot better than I did a minute ago. 'What are we going to do now?'

'Well, we have a couple options.'

'That's more than I thought of.'

'What did you think of?' he spells.

'That I'd run up to him and throw the grenade at him.'

'That's probably not the best idea.'

'Probably not, but how else am I going to get him and the grenade together?'

'Here's a thought. You could leave it with me, and I could throw it at him.'

I shake my head. 'I like that idea even less.'

'Well, I don't like my other thoughts.'

'Why not?'

'They put you in even more danger than you're already in.'

I give his hand a squeeze. 'I don't know how that can be. Living the way I do, knowing what's to come...' I put my free hand on the mark I know mars my neck. 'There's not much else you can do to me.'

'I know. I just wish it didn't have to be this way.'

'So what's your other idea?' I spell.

'Ideas. One, you could hide in the servants' entrance and throw the grenade at him when he goes in his room.'

'Not much different than my idea.'

'But this way you'd be hidden. You could roll the grenade in the room while he isn't looking.'

'Hm. That would be better than just throwing it at him. It still gives me the jeebees, though.'

'Maybe my second idea will work. We tie a string around the pin of the grenade, and attach it to the door of his room. This way, when he enters the room, the grenade will go off, and you won't have to be anywhere near him when it does.'

A knowing feeling settles through me. 'This is it. This is how we should do it.'

'It's still dangerous for you.'

'It's dangerous, no matter what. I think this posseses the least amount of risk.' I let my words dissolve and then add, 'I'll do it tomorrow.'

'Is it enough time to warn everyone away?'

'It has to be. I'm afraid if we give them too much time, someone will slip and the word will get back to your father.'

'Tomorrow it is.'

'I'd better go and start spreading the word.'

He pulls me closer before I can get away. 'You be careful now. All right?'

'Of course I will. I'll do everything I can to make this happen while still staying safe.' I just hope it works.

CHAPTER 46

I tie the string around the doorknob and pull tight—a little too tight for comfort, as it leads to a grenade. The grenade sits in a stand. A second one is also attached to the door, better hidden behind it than the first. Between the two of them, the blast should leave nothing of the Grand Chancellor .

I wish there was a way to test them out, but of course it's not possible. I can only hope they're set up well enough.

I move to leave by the way of the servants' entrance but stop. There's not time to delay—the Grand Chancellor could come back at any time—but what if it doesn't work? What if the door opens and the grenades fall out of their containers instead of exploding? What if something else goes wrong?

Nathaniel said he thinks his father can track spells, but he can't track them if he's dead.

I swallow and stop hesitating. I run for the nearest grenade, trying to keep my footsteps silent. As soon as I get there, I cast a spell on both grenades to cause a bigger explosion and add some fire when the door opens. This is easier than doing an explosion from scratch.

The spells are vivid red, fiery orange, and yellow. They'll definitely be spotted by anyone who comes in the servants' entrance, but barring anything bad, there shouldn't be anyone coming through the servants' entrance. Oh please, don't let anything go wrong with this.

I make my way out and hope against all hope that everything goes smoothly. My heart is pounding like a mad woman's as I make my way away from the Grand Chancellor's rooms. The farther I get, the more confident I feel with not getting caught immediately, but the more fear I have about something going wrong.

What if I cast the wrong spell? What if the pins don't come out of the grenade, or the spell doesn't set them off? What if the Grand Chancellor doesn't make his way to his rooms like he usually does? So much could go wrong.

I make it to the kitchen, where Three is waiting for me.

"Are you ready for a walk?" she asks me.

'Did you warn all the tarnished?' I spell out in a green and yellow.

She nods.

Good. I wish we could warn the regular servants too, but with people like Fredrick, that's impossible. The Grand Chancellor would know what we're up to for sure if he doesn't notice that suddenly all the chores aren't getting done. There are so many ifs, but I have to believe this will work. "Yes, let's go. Right now."

Being around another person is comforting, but I still don't trust that everything is going to go right.

What I've done hasn't hit yet. Tarnished are gathered outside, staring up at the house. I join them, Three at my side. If the Grand Chancellor looks out the window right now, he's going to wonder what is going on. Maybe I was wrong to warn everyone, but I can't have their lives on my hands. I can't become as bad as the Grand Chancellor himself.

A few other tarnished trickle out of the house to us. Still we wait, and nothing happens. Maybe I did something wrong. I didn't leave the string right, or the grenades malfunctioned. Failure is growing more likely by the moment, and each moment that ticks by is another the Grand Chancellor lives.

There's a *boom* coming from the Grand Chancellor's rooms and an explosion of fire and smoke.

I did it. We did it. I roll my shoulders into a relaxed position. I can't help the smile that comes to the corner of my mouth. Now to make sure the fire doesn't spread to other parts of the house, and then to go meet up with Nathaniel. He should be free now that his father is dead. Thank goodness his room is far away from his father's. All rooms are far from his father's. It's like the man doesn't trust anyone close to him.

He's dead. I can't believe I did it. My heart clenches to know I killed someone. To know I made another person die. But I can't help feeling like it is supposed to be this way, even if his death is now on my hands. It's a price I'm willing to pay, to get rid of such evil scum.

But really, I need to make certain he's dead and then put out the fire, and I need to do it now. I take a step forward. From somewhere behind me, a blue-lighted spell flashes through the air, heading straight for the fire eating at the Grand Chancellor's rooms. Someone beat me to putting out the fire.

I turn around to see who it is. My lungs collapse. It's the Grand Chancellor.

CHAPTER 47

"Well, well, well," he says. "What have we here? A group of tarnished stand out on my lawn, watching my house burn. And not just any part of my house, but my rooms."

He pauses, looking us all over. I keep my head down, but I can feel his gaze raking over me. He knows I caused this. He has to. What have I done? What trouble have I caused that I shouldn't have? Who set off the explosion? What will happen to me now? What will happen to the others?

I realize my hands are shaking. I fist them at my sides. I can't lose control of myself. Not in front of him. If there's something he doesn't know yet, I can't let it out. I have to keep all my secrets. Why didn't I think this out better? Nathaniel was right. I shouldn't have tried.

Why is the Grand Chancellor still not saying anything else?

I chance a peek at him through my lashes. He's staring straight at me. I lower my head and bite my lip.

"Some of you seem to think you can get away with whatever you want. You didn't learn the lesson last time of keeping your business where it belongs. Of what happens to those who go against me."

Suddenly, Three is screaming, a horrifying screeching sound.

I run to her arching body, but before I can reach her, she flies up in the air like Cook did before the Grand Chancellor killed him. A horrible sinking feeling rocks through me. The Grand Chancellor must think Three started the fire, not I. He's punishing her for the crime I committed.

I turn toward him, to tell him it was me. That he's made a mistake. But he's already watching me, a knowing smile on his face.

He's knows it was me who did it, and he's torturing Three because of me. Probably because he wants to save me for the sacrifice. This can't be happening.

I look up at Three in the air, still screaming. It's a heart wrenching sound.

What have I done?

I hover close by under her, wishing there was a way I could get to her, to give her some sort of comfort. But by her cries, I'm not sure anything can help at this point. I'd use magic, but if the whole group of Sanos couldn't defeat him, what good would I do? The screaming continues on and on. I realize I'm crying. Three's screams are losing their strength. They become more and more pitiful, though her back is still arched like she's being tormented.

Finally, she flops to the ground. I try to catch her, but miss. I end up on the ground beside her, checking for a pulse.

Nothing.

"You think you can get away with whatever you want," the Grand Chancellor says. I look up and he's staring right at me again. Chills course through me as he continues. "You can't get away with anything."

With that, he storms back to the house. There's barely any time to think of the fact that he didn't torture or threaten the rest of us more. If he was really aiming at just me, he did enough. Being present for Three's torture was worse than when he tortured us in the ballroom.

I grab Three's hand. It's completely lifeless. I bend down and whisper in her ear, "I'm sorry. I'm so, so sorry."

CHAPTER 48

I stand in Nathaniel's room, numb to anything. We buried
Three and had a short service for her right after the Grand
Chancellor left. There wasn't time to do anything proper. The
Grand Chancellor thinks he's won, and… well… he's right.

I will remember Three forever. Her sweet spirit, her ideas, and
her love for Abby. I'll also remember how hard I failed her. How
it's my fault she's gone. The only consolation I have is that she
lived this life so long and hated it. There was nothing she wanted
to do with it at all. Now, she doesn't have to. Still, the tears fall.

Nathaniel doesn't say a word. Doesn't spell anything out. He
wraps his arms around me. I rest my head against his chest and
just cry and cry. The sharp torment in my chest is never going to
leave. I've let myself and everyone else down.

He rubs my back, soothing my frayed nerves. I start to calm
down, but the pain doesn't lessen. I don't think it ever will.

'What happened?' he spells out.

'Plan failed.'

'I figured that when the spells on my room didn't go away.
What else happened?'

'Three. My dear friend. She was…' A sob chokes out of me.

188

He makes circles on my back, giving me time to compose myself.

When I can, I spell out in deep blue letters, 'She was tortured and killed in my place.'

'My father thought it was her who tried to kill him?'

'Oh no. I saw the look on his face. He knows I'm the one who did it. I think he's letting me live because he wants to make a sacrifice of me in front of everyone. It's funny to think my imminent death saved my life a little longer, but that it was at Three's expense... I just can't.'

'It's all right. I'm here.'

And he is. For the whole time we usually spend cleaning his room, all the time I might spend napping or having a spelled conversation with him, he just holds me.

When it's almost time to go, he spells out, 'Do you know who caused the explosion if it wasn't him?'

'Not for certain, but there's one tarnished missing. The one whose tattoos looked sort of like a cat's.'

'Bless her soul.'

Exactly. When all this happened, I never thought another tarnished would be the victim of my plans. It shouldn't have to be this way. To make things worse, the way he treated Three afterward, knowing it was me who should have been in her place the entire time.

'Why does he have to be so harsh?'

He shakes his head. 'I don't know. I can't understand how his hatred for women and those he thinks are less than him has grown so deep he has to act in this way. I only hope I can figure out a way to keep you safe.'

'It's too late at this point. Nothing can save me now.'

'Who knows? Maybe I can get close enough to him that I can do something.'

'It's so risky. He seems to know everything. Do you think he knows about us?'

'No. If he knew about us, he'd put a stop to it. He'd never stand for me having a relationship with a tarnished. It's just not allowed in his world.'

I rest my head on his shoulder, utterly spent. 'At least we have each other for however short a time we have left together before the sacrifice.' I stand and turn to leave the room.

Before I can go, he spells out in bright yellow before me. 'I will do whatever I can to save your life. I promise you. If I can stop your sacrifice, I will.'

I turn back to him and give him a smile devoid of joy. 'I know you will.' But it won't be enough. I am going to die.

CHAPTER 49

"You won't need to take Nathaniel a dinner plate," Fredrick, the head servant, says.

"Oh?" What could have happened to cause this catastrophe?

"He and the Grand Chancellor have made up, and they are going to have dinner together."

Now that is a good reason. Hopefully he's making a lot of progress with his father. "Does his room still need to be cleaned?"

"Yes. You can fit that into your chores whenever tonight, as long as you don't disturb Nathaniel's sleep."

"Of course." I hurry away from Fredrick, glad to be far from him.

I get on with my chores, trying not to hum. This is a very good development. Better yet, I get to pick when I fit cleaning his room into my schedule, so I can make sure he's there, and not have to clean it while he's gone to dinner, like the Grand Chancellor insists we do with his room.

As I walk through the hall, I hear someone coming. I slide to the side of the wall like I'm supposed to and try to become as small as possible. Like nothing but a speck of dust. When it's Nathaniel that walks by with the Grand Chancellor, I can't help but smile. Until I see the guards with them. The Grand Chancellor always has guards. I thought he'd let up on them with Nathaniel around. How is Nathaniel supposed to make a move now?

A few hours later, I make my way to Nathaniel's rooms for cleaning. Or really, to see how things went at dinner. And just to be close to him. I missed him at our usual meeting time, and it's making it hard to think of my chores.

His room is empty when I enter. I scowl at my luck. I thought for sure they'd be done with dinner by now. The Grand Chancellor must have kept him to do something more than just eat. I should have waited longer, instead of being so eager to see him. Better yet, I shouldn't have encouraged him to make friends with his father, not only putting him in more danger, but keeping him away longer.

The spells are off his room at least. Maybe he'll be allowed to move around freely. That would be a good change for him.

I get to work, scrubbing away. It's not ideal. Everything reminds me of Nathaniel, at my side, helping. Whether we work in silence or send messages to each other, it's a soothing process compared to the rest of my day. One I'm sorely missing.

Nathaniel comes in his room, and I smile, until I see his father with him. Immediately I tense, remembering what happened last time he was here. I keep cleaning but edge toward the water closet so I won't have to remain in the same room with him.

"Thank you for dinner," Nathaniel says.

"If your attitude remains positive, we share one again." With that, the Grand Chancellor leaves, and my muscles relax. At least he hardly stayed at all. As soon as the door closes, though, the lock-down spell zips through the room again. Guess the experiment is still a work in progress.

Nathaniel falls on his bed and doesn't move. I keep cleaning, unsure he even knows I'm here, as well as to give him a little space for the moment.

'It's good to see you,' he spells out, zipping it over to the corner where I'm currently working. So he knows I'm here.

I move over to him. 'It's even better to see you. How did dinner go? You were gone longer than I expected.'

He shakes his head and falls back onto the bed. A moment later, he zips out another spell that hovers right above him. 'Horrible. It's going to take a long time to earn his trust. If I ever earn it at all. There's no chance I'll be able to attack him while in this house. His guards follow him everywhere.'

'I'm sorry things didn't go better. Hopefully they will with time.'

'Time is the one thing you don't have.'

Don't I know it?

CHAPTER 50

A week later, I go into Nathaniel's room, unsure if he's going to be there or not. He's been gone much of the week with the Grand Chancellor. Though usually I'm told if dinner doesn't need taken to him, and this time I've heard nothing. I'm hopeful I'll get to see him. To hear if things are going any better.

I don't see anyone when I open the door. My heart sinks. Oh, well. This was the plan. He's supposed to be making nice with his father. This has to mean it's working.

I move farther into the room, only to find him lounging on the couch. He pops up as soon as he sees me, but the look on his face is grim.

'Bad news?' I spell to him.

He sighs and flops back down on the couch. I hurry to his side and kneel on the ground next to the couch. 'What happened?'

'My father. What else?'

What else, indeed. I give him a moment, figuring he'll talk about it when he's ready. I stay close, hoping to calm him with my presence. If it can do any calming. At this point, I'm not even sure.

Finally, he spells out, 'My father will never trust me. Not in time. I've done too much in the past to go against him.'

I grab his hand and give it a squeeze.

He sits up and guides me to the couch next to him. I curl up and lean my head on his shoulder, while he puts an arm around me.

'My father says he appreciates all I'm trying to do, reaching out to him, but he never tells his guards to give us privacy.'

'But that's nothing new, right?' I spell back. 'We figured you wouldn't be able to do him in yourself.'

'Yes, but it's frustrating. And today he said that, despite the efforts I've made, he just can't trust me at a critical time such as this.'

My heart drops. There's no use. What else can we possibly do to defeat the Grand Chancellor when he doesn't even trust his own son? That's it, then.

He pulls me closer and kisses the top of my head. I snuggle into him, not caring if any of my work gets done. What's the point? Not only am I cleaning a room that's already clean, but if there's no way to get on the Grand Chancellor's good side, I'm as good as dead anyway.

It doesn't have to be this way. Not really. I sit upright, energy pulsing through me. Nathaniel gives me a curious look.

'What's the one thing he won't see coming?' I spell.

'I don't know. What?'

'Me.'

CHAPTER 51

Planning. It's the only thing I have left to do, besides getting rid of the Grand Chancellor himself. The first thing I need to do is get a note to Serena and get Katherine involved. Only thing standing in my way is Fredrick. Literally.

"What do you think you're doing?" he demands.

"Going for a walk."

"Tarnished don't go for walks."

I try to keep my voice civil. Lashing out wouldn't work right now, but it's terribly hard not to. "It's my free time. There's nothing left for me to do but sleep. I think it's my own choice if I get sleep or not."

He moves in, leering down on me. The note in my pocket feels as if it weighs thousands of pounds. It yanks and pulls at me. What if he finds it? What if he realizes what I'm actually doing?

"Tarnished don't get to do whatever they want. If you think there's time to go for a walk instead of sleep, then we'll just add some more chores to your list, shall we?"

Please, no. The last thing I need is more stuff to do. "I'm sorry. I will head up to bed now."

"Ah, ah, ah. I don't think so. Go mop the kitchen floor."

I bite back a retort. It's then I realize how strong I've become. I would never have had a retort before. Instead, I would have meekly gone and done what was asked of me. And the only reason I'm biting back the retort now is I know what's best for me. I have to keep myself out of trouble if I'm going to have this plan succeed.

"Yes, sir." But I still need to get my note sent out. I don't know how much time they need, but I know the tournament is very, very close. Probably within the week. There's no time to delay.

But Fredrick doesn't move. He stands there scowling down at me, nostrils flaring. "Get a move on."

I turn and take a few steps. When I glance back, he's still watching me. I'll have to find another way to get the note out.

I make my way to the kitchen, immediately missing Cook the moment I step in. His screams still haunt me. What's more, I miss his kindness. If he were here, I could ask him to hide the note for me. It would mean giving away my secret, but it would be worth it for this final note. This happens every time I come in the kitchen.

I get the supplies and begin mopping the floor, only to find Fredrick has followed me to the kitchen. He's merciless. Why won't he just leave me alone?

He moves to me and pushes my head toward the ground. "You missed a spot."

I clench back my words and scrub the spot he's talking about. After several more minutes of scouring, he says, "You'd better keep this up. I don't want to see a single speck of dirt on the floor next time I'm in here."

With that, he stomps out of the room.

Like there's a speck of dirt on it now. I don't know why he's so uptight about these things. If only he were on our side instead of fighting against us.

I'm quick to finish mopping, not caring how good a job I do. The floor didn't need to be mopped in the first place. My doing it again isn't going to make a difference. Once finished, I wonder if I dare go back out there. I have to, though. It's difficult to know how much time I have for certain, but it's not long. I need to get this message out.

I creep back outside, ready to claim I'm going to the outhouse, should Fredrick reappear. Thankfully, he doesn't. I scan the area for any wondering eyes, but there's not a soul out here. I hurry to place the note in its hiding spot and cover it up. As I move toward the tarnished bedroom, I hope the note is picked up soon and Serena can do what needs to be done.

CHAPTER 52

As soon as my chores are finished for the day, I make my way to the laundry room, usually the best place to find Tawny. I guess with her height, putting her anywhere else makes it hard to hide her as a shadow. Not to mention the steel that shines from her eyes. She's a tarnished that's nothing like a tarnished. Even less so than Katherine.

I'm happy to find she's there and I don't have to hunt her down in her room. It's much harder to talk to her there. Only thing is, two other tarnished are here right now, so I can't spell whatever message I want to Tawny.

With a sigh, I settle in next to her to do some laundry. Of course I have to do extra chores, instead of telling her what I need and going to bed. At least I'm doing something. If this doesn't work, soon I won't be doing chores or sleeping.

Half an hour of scrubbing later, the two other tarnished finally leave.

'I didn't think they would ever go,' Tawny spells.

'Me either.'

'What's going on?'

Leave it to her to get right to business. 'I have a huge favor to ask.'

'Of course. What is it?'

'I need you to find a way to give me the califrasum before the tournament.'

'That's a tall order. Why am I feeding you a drug that will make you obey others around you?'

'Because that's not what you're really going to give me. If you can find a way to be in charge of giving it to me, you can switch it for something innocent. Something that won't make me docile.'

Her smile brightens. 'I'll do whatever I can to make it happen.'

CHAPTER 53

I t's so good to see Katherine again. I can't say so or spell it with other people around, but it's good. She hands me a basket of food, which I take into the house. By the time I get back out there, the food is all in the house, and she's helping the driver load up to go. Except there's one more package. With a quick glance around, she hands the package to me. It's thin enough to slip in my shirt, but I'll soon have to find somewhere to keep it.

She gives my hand a squeeze, and then she's off. The cart rolls away with her sitting by the driver, neither looking back at me. How I wish I could jump on that cart and go with them, but if I did, I'd be just as dead as I will be after being sacrificed. Only this time with no hope of survival. No hope others might finally be free if I take the smallest chance to defeat the Grand Chancellor.

A knot forms in my chest. I hurry away before it creeps to my eyes and turns to tears. That was my last chore of the day, so I head to the outhouse—the only place to get privacy. The best place I have to look at the package Katherine gave me.

As soon as I close the door, the package is out and I'm ripping it open. The material is white and thin. Not much to it. But then, I suppose a sacrifice doesn't need much. My only problem is I can't find a hidden pocket. Did she forget?

I run my hands across the seams on the side again. Nothing on the left side. I search the right and finally find it. Clever. She sewed it into the seam, and it's barely wide enough for me to reach in.

The extra things I need are here as well. Katherine delivered.

Maybe, just maybe, I'll be able to pull this off.

* * *

IT'S the last night before the tournament. Tomorrow I'll be sacrificed right in front of Nathaniel and my family if there's nothing I can do to stop it. I know my mother and sisters will make it there. I only wonder what they'll do if I fail. There's no chance the Grand Chancellor will let them get away. Not again.

I shake the negative thoughts away and walk into Nathaniel's room. He's there, waiting for me in the middle of the room. I hurry to shut the door behind me and rush into his arms. There'll be no cleaning his room today. I doubt anyone will notice, but even if they did, I'll be gone.

He pulls me close, rubbing my back. I wrap my arms around him, wishing I never had to let go. My eyes burn. Now is the only time I have to break down. The only chance to let my emotions out about what's to happen. What's likely to happen. Plans fail.

Nathaniel just holds me, and I hold him.

I wish I could say goodbye to my sisters and Waverly as well. But there won't be a chance. The best I can do is send them a note.

'Everything will be fine,' he spells to me.

I hope he's right.

CHAPTER 54

My nerves sputter, like they are dying. I'm at the tournament, waiting alone in a tent for my time to either die or live. I pace back and forth, allowing the memory of Zade. If I don't succeed, my life won't be the only one forfeited this night. Many count on me and Tawny to get this right. I have to make it work. We both do. And if I fail...

It doesn't matter. I can't think like that. The little tent I'm waiting in is void of anything, making it hard to find a distraction. The minutes tick on and on, leaving me feeling like I'm going to die of old age before it's finally time to come get me. To lead me to be sacrificed.

A tarnished comes in. Not Tawny. I clamp my mouth shut in fear, wondering what could have happened to her. She worked hard at being trusted with this job. Why is another tarnished here?

Another thought hits me, brutal and harsh. What if they caught her in what she was doing? What if she's already dead because of me?

I can't have her life on my hands. Though I suppose, if I fail—which it looks like I'm going to—I will be seeing her soon if she's already been killed. My heart feels as if it's nowhere to be found. It's stopped beating. What have I done?

The tarnished isn't one I've seen before. He moves forward, a glass in his hand filled with a pale brown liquid. I bite my lip, wishing it hadn't come to this. If I refuse to drink it, what will happen?

As if reading my thoughts, the tarnished says, "I need you to drink this. If you don't, you'll be forced to, and it won't be pretty."

I stare at the glass, wondering if it's worth it to fight. If it'd do any good.

But of course it won't. I'm already doomed. Maybe I can fight the califrasum. What I should have been doing this entire time was building up immunity to it, not relying on someone switching it for something harmless. It was a stupid move that will end in not only my death, but also the death of countless others and the continued rule of a madman.

The tarnished takes a step forward.

I take a step back.

"Are you going to make me call the guards?" he asks.

I shake my head but still take another step back.

"Come on, now. You need to drink this without delay, or I'll be in trouble as well."

He knows my weakness. I step forward until I can take the glass from his hands. It's heavy with the weight of my failure. Heavy with the thought of all those I've let down.

"No more stalling," he says.

I put the glass to my lips and chug down the contents, trying not to think how much it tastes like dirt. Soon I will be under the control of others, unable to do anything for myself. Unless I can fight it, which I don't know how to do. Wasn't prepared to do. I should have come up with a different plan, for this one has surely failed me.

How long does it take to work? The tarnished watches me. Am I going to do something different when it kicks in? Will I know?

Serena once talked about the effects of it. Of how horrid it was. Of how she had to do exactly what anyone said. I will watch myself go willingly to my own death.

A sort of numbness washes over me. Whatever comes will come. I can only try my best to do what needs to be done, and if I can't, it's no longer under my control. Not that much ever was; I just wanted to think I was doing some good.

I hope my sisters know how much I love them. How much I've missed them while I've been captured. And Nathaniel... I've slowly gotten to know him more. My heart yearns to be with him. To have his arms wrapped around me again, keeping me safe. But nothing can keep me safe from what's to come.

A guard sticks his head in the opening of the tent. "It's time. Bring her."

The tarnished walks over to me and says, "You will follow me."

And so I do. Whether it's of my own volition or because of the califrasum, I can't tell. All I know is this is where I'm supposed to go. This is where I'll lose my life.

CHAPTER 55

The tournament grounds are dark. Much different than I remember from when Cynthia battled. Boxes and stands all around the field are full of people. Part of me hopes Serena, Cynthia, and Waverly are here somewhere, hiding. The rest of me fears the same thing. What if I don't succeed? It's likely I won't. What will happen to them if they're caught?

I try to act as emotionless as I remember the sacrifice being that time. Try to pretend that califrasum is working, but it's difficult with all the memories flooding me of the tarnished led to her death so blandly.

And I have to do the same.

Despite the weight in the hidden pocket of my shift, there's no guarantee I'll come out of this alive. No guarantee I will succeed. Many others have tried before me and failed. I don't know what will be different this time, but I'm determined to do my best.

"Move forward and get on the stone slab," one of my guards calls out. "No fighting once there."

I hurry to comply before I can tell if my body will betray me. As I move onto the field, my heart cries out. Nathaniel stands next to his father. Both of them are between the stone slab and their prisoners.

Zade and Daniel look worse than when I last saw them. They're thinner, more frail looking. Plus, their bodies are covered in bruises. The sight hurts my chest. If I fail, my death won't be the only one.

The field is dark except for a few torchlights setup along the path. The stone I'm to be sacrificed on is clean of blood. Even though I know how valuable blood magic is, I still expected to see some spilled. Some hint of what has happened before. The thought makes me queasy.

The stone itself is big enough to easily fit me. Up close, I realize a part of it juts out like a step.

I climb on the sacrificial stone and settle on it like I don't have a care in the world. Like the stone isn't freezing. And like I'm not waiting for my death.

It's smooth beneath me. Smooth and hard and cold.

The Grand Chancellor leers over me, like he's hungry for my magic. Probably wishes I had as much as Cynthia, but any magic will add to his horde. I try to stare vacantly up at the sky, but it's hard not to react to him hovering over me.

He casts a spell—a thin, dull-gray one with spots of sparkling yellow. It takes the shape of a knife and moves toward my arm. I focus on the sky and on controlling my breathing. Slow breaths in, slow breaths out. Inhaling the clean night air. Letting out the taint of having the Grand Chancellor about to steal my magic and my life.

There's a sharp prick on my arm. Thankfully I was expecting it so I don't react, but it stings. The Grand Chancellor casts a spell on his own arm, before pricking it as well. He casts a third spell that moves toward me in a serpentine fashion, sparkling gold.

I clench my jaw as the spell moves ever closer until it touches me. I can't suppress the shiver that runs through me, but the

Grand Chancellor doesn't seem to notice. He's fully focused on my blood. The spell pulls my blood toward him.

There's a yanking deep inside me. It's small at first but grows with the flow of my life's blood. The more it yanks and pulls, the more I want to fight against it. The more I want to scream at him to stop. No wonder the women are drugged first. Sitting though this without reacting is maddening. The tugging on my magic is worse than losing my life's force.

Though the Grand Chancellor is focused wholly on my arm, on the magic he's stealing from me, his eyes are clear. I don't dare try to kill him yet, for fear the slightest movement will disturb him.

The world starts to darken further than just the night sky. I'm losing myself, but the Grand Chancellor is focused on me. I force myself to stay awake, even as my eyelids turn heavy. Still, I hang on. I fight against the blackness. Fight against losing myself. Not just yet.

Thoughts flash through my mind. Of Serena gaining her freedom. Of Cynthia winning the tournament. Of Waverly leading us to war. Of my sisters. Of Nathaniel.

Too many thoughts pull me in, and I long to lose myself in memories. My breath comes in shallow gasps. I'm going. This will kill me, whether I succeed or not. The thought saddens me for only a moment. If I'm going to die, I hope to die doing the best I can.

I can't wait any longer. I have to risk it. My hand doesn't want to follow my command to move. I take several deep breaths and get ready to go through the movements as fast and accurately as I can.

For a moment, I feel sorry for the Grand Chancellor. Not for what he's done, but for the person he's become. For the hate he's spread. If only he could have been better, I wouldn't have to do this. I wouldn't have to become a person I don't want to be. The world grows darker around the edges.

I grab the gun from my hidden pocket and point it at the Grand Chancellor. As I put pressure on the trigger, he widens his eyes. Everything seems to slow.

The tugging on my magic stops.

The world fades out as my body tries to force me to sleep.

Blood spills across my arm, wetting the stone around me.

The Grand Chancellor reaches up.

I focus on his chest.

There's screaming.

I pull the trigger.

The world blurs.

I give my life in exchange for his death.

This sacrifice of mine.

Everything is dark.

Serena

CHAPTER 56

I'm moving before Bethany even pulls the trigger, racing down the stairs of the box we were hiding in. The sound of a gun echoes through the air as I land on the ground and run. People are screaming. Bethany is limp on the stone and so, so pale.

Memories of the first time I saw a sacrifice flash through me. How cold and dark the tarnished was. Just like Bethany is now.

I push myself faster.

The Grand Chancellor stumbles. Guards are at his side, and suddenly, Zade is at mine. I don't even have time to enjoy the feel of his hand in mine, only to notice his grip isn't as strong as it should be, before we reach the stone.

I grab Bethany's hand, but it flops. Zade rips part of his tattered shirt and presses it against her wound. But there's already so much blood everywhere, not to mention all the Grand Chancellor already stole.

Bethany is so very cold.

There's no life left in her. I sob, aching for my sister.

There's a noise to my left. I turn to see my father barreling toward me. Never seen a fat man run so fast. Anger sears my entire body. It's partly his fault all of this happened. If he were a good father, we wouldn't be in this situation.

I pull as much of my magic as possible toward my center and release it in a burst of icy-blue flares. They slam into him and cover his body before he can do anything about it.

"Cynthia," I yell. "*Get him.*"

Cynthia

CHAPTER 57

As soon as the trigger goes off, I'm up. I throw myself over the side of the box, zapping a spell out to catch myself before I fall to the ground. As I move to run, I trip. *Blasted skirts.*

I'm on my feet again. Serena is already at the stone, with Zade at her side. By the way she's crying, I know it's too late, but I refuse to believe it. Not Bethany. This war can't take her. It just can't.

Serena turns and zaps a blue spell to the left side of her. I follow it to find father encased in a freezing spell.

"Cynthia. Get him," Serena yells.

No problem. I've been waiting to do this my entire life.

I pull together everything I have and thrust a sleeping spell at him, knocking him to the ground. I only wish I had it in me to kill him after everything he's done.

I keep running and reach Bethany's side to find Zade pressing a dirty cloth to her arm. I rip a large chuck off cloth off my skirt and move his hand.

When I take off the dirty rag, I find a long, deep cut, oozing blood. I press the skirt cloth against the wound and hold it there, but still, she doesn't stir.

Her face is so pale, I can't imagine her making it through this. I keep the cloth pressed down anyway and look around, wondering why no one has tried to stop us yet.

The Grand Chancellor's guards are hovering over him, fully focused on him and nothing else. The crowd is in chaos, screaming and running, but the only one rushing toward us is Waverly. For the first time since Bethany first lay down on the stone, a tiny light of hope springs in me. Waverly knows how to heal. She can fix her. She has to.

"Hurry," I call out to her.

At last, the guards seem to realize what we're doing. One of them turns to see Waverly coming our way. He zips a spell toward us.

"Hold this," I say to Serena.

As soon as her hand is on the cloth, I'm racing toward Waverly like my life depends on it. No, like Bethany's life depends on it. Before I get there, I zap the guard.

He slams to the ground and doesn't get up again. No one else dares to get in Waverly's way once they see me.

But for all my skills, I can't put life back into Bethany.

Waverly

CHAPTER 58

A s soon as Cynthia clears the way for me, I'm by Bethany's
side. I take her pulse. Nothing. I wait and try not to look
into the faces of those around me.

Still nothing. Then the faintest of faint movements. And then
another, but too weak. "She's alive, but she needs help," I say.

I shove away from the stone, heading for the Grand Chancellor. I only hope he's not too far gone. I take his pulse. Though his
eyes are closed and he's not moving, it's there. Muted, but there. I
cast a spell, pulling at the wound he opened to take Bethany's
blood.

"What are you doing?" Serena asks.

"She needs blood."

"How can we help?" Cynthia asks.

"Pray this works."

After uncovering Bethany's wound, I pull the blood from the
Grand Chancellor and put in back in Bethany through the wound
in her arm. There's no way to know if I'm doing this right. I've
never done anything like this before. It has to work, though. It just
has to.

My heart pounds hard, like it's trying to break free from my chest. Beside me, the Grand Chancellor's pulse goes from barely there to not there at all. I don't know how much longer I can give Bethany back her blood if he's dead. I stop, hoping it's enough.

She's still. Oh-so still.

Serena

CHAPTER 59

Father appears behind Cynthia. I rush over and smash my gun against his head. It doesn't work as well as my first hit did. Instead of getting knocked out, he staggers back. I point the gun toward him, aiming for his chest.

Cynthia moves, getting in the way of my shot.

I realize the field is flooding with people. Not just Chardonias, but Envadi. Even a few Chryons. Law officers are turning on the rebels. People on the crowd are turning on them, but more people are turning on the law officers.

My chest swells. It's happening. The Grand Chancellor is gone, and the people are turning on those who've oppressed them this long. With the help of foreigners, we'll win. I know we will.

Cynthia twists toward father, and I turn to Zade. He leans against me heavily. I didn't realize just how weak he is until this moment. I know he has been through a lot, but to have his tall frame touching mine, I can feel how thin he's grown. His bones poke through his ribs.

I wrap my arm around him, supporting him. A law officer comes straight for us. Without a thought, I thrust a wall spell at him. He slams against it with such force he falls to the ground.

"That's my girl," Zade whispers.

My heart soars. I turn and zap another law officer nearby and another. I can do this. I can fight with magic.

Cynthia

CHAPTER 60

My father smirks at me like he doesn't think I can do anything against him. That, or he doesn't think I will. Whichever it is, he's mistaken. I raise my hand toward him.

He immediately throws up a shield. "You don't belong on this field," he yells at me.

"Neither do you." I zap a hammering spell at his wall, trying to take it down. For every block my silver spell chips away, another piece of black wall takes its place. The wall is thicker than I've encountered before.

Despite growing up with his punishments, I didn't expect him to be so strong. No wonder his daughters have so much magic. No wonder I do. I'm not about to thank him for it. Instead, I thrust my spell harder toward him.

His spell finally lessens, no longer recuperating as fast as I take it down. As soon as there's a chink big enough, I zap a stunning spell through his wall. As it nears him, he shoots up a yellow spell that collides with mine in a burst.

Hoping to use the element of surprise, I run at him. Before I reach him, I stop and let the rest of my momentum out through my hand, in a spell that's a sharp obsidian black. He dodges it, but stumbles back. I thrust another and another at him. He spells up a shield, but my spells slice into it like it's nothing before they run out of energy.

For the first time in my life, I think I may actually be stronger then him. He sends a flaming spell at me. I dodge to the left, but not fast enough. The spell hits me on the thigh. The scent of scorched flesh fills the air. I bite my lip and shoot my own flaming spell, smaller than father's was, but hotter. When it's halfway to him, it splits into three, the middle one going straight for him, while the outer two each take a side.

He takes a step back.

Finally, I have him right where I want him.

Bethany

CHAPTER 61

M y body aches. Why am I in such pain? And why am I so cold? Someone takes hold of my hand. Someone else is crying. What is going on?

I blink. It's harder than I expected it to be.

Screams all around me. I open my eyes to find Nathaniel hovering close by. His hand is on mine, but he faces away from me, casting a spell.

He turns back. As soon as he sees me, he gasps. "You're alive. We all thought you were dead."

"I'm alive," I choke out. I cough and look about.

People are fighting. The place is a mess of screaming and flashing colors. The fight looks strong. People are everywhere, angry looks across their faces. It's clear the law officers are losing. They cower against spells from all sides. What's more, father is cringing away from Cynthia. She looks about to cast a spell at him as another hovers around him, flaming.

"Stop," I croak out.

No one listens.

I force myself to my feet and spell my voice to be heard above the din. "Stop."

The fighting comes to a halt. Cynthia still aims her hand at father, but she looks at me, relief etched on her features. Near me, Serena and Zade also look just as relieved. Waverly, Lukas, Jack, and Katherine are all nearby. They're all looking at me, as if I've risen from the dead. Which it feels like I have.

Everyone stares at me, not just they. I realize this is it—I have one moment to stop the fighting before it goes any further. Before more lives are lost.

"Now is not the time for fighting," I say. "Now is the time to put aside our differences and accept that everyone has equal rights. If you can't accept it, fine, but you are no longer welcome in Chardonia. If you choose to stay and treat others as if they are worth less than you, consequences will befall you."

Some cheers rouse through the air, and then the fighting starts back up. Not on a grand scale, just a few skirmishes here and there. The people don't seem to like it, though. Those closest, whose expressions I can make out, are glaring at those law officers still trying to fight. But mostly, the crowd goes silent.

My knees quiver. I glance at Cynthia, for guidance. She looks at father. He raises his hand toward her, but she's quicker, flashing a spell that hits him square in the chest. He falls to the ground, but his chest is still moving. There are a few gasps from bystanders, yet she keeps on moving.

She joins me up on the sacrificial rock and holds me steady. "The fighting ends now." Her voice echoes through the field.

The people cheer and run toward the law officers left standing. A few flashes of color appear, but they mostly come from law officers, giving themselves up. I sit back down on the rock and close my eyes. I'm so very tired. Nathaniel takes me into his arms and cradles me close to his chest. I drift off.

CHAPTER 62

I wake back up to still being held by Nathaniel.

"She's awake," Serena says.

The crying grows stronger. Serena puts a hand on my shoulder. Cynthia is holding my hand. To my right side, Waverly moves toward me like she's seen a ghost, her face pale.

"What happened?"

"You did it," Cynthia says.

"Did what?"

"You defeated the Grand Chancellor." Waverly's voice holds a note of awe I never heard before.

Relief fills me. Nathaniel bends down and presses a kiss to my forehead. "I thought you were dead. I thought I lost you."

"But you didn't."

"I think we missed something," Cynthia says.

And I laugh. *Laugh.* The sound is unfamiliar, coming from my lips. It's rusty with disuse, but it's still there.

When I finally stop laughing, I say, "Nathaniel is important to me." I look him right in the eye. "He's the man I love."

He bends down and kisses me on the lips. I kiss him back, not caring how many people are here to see it. His warmth is much needed and a direct contrast to the cold I'm feeling.

After we pull apart, I say, "Can someone help me off of this stone? It's freezing."

Nathaniel doesn't hesitate to take me into his arms and pull me off the stone. I shudder as I leave it, not knowing if I'll ever be the same again. I doubt anything will ever be the same again. Hopefully, most change is for the best, but I don't know if I will be better for it or not.

The crowd around us is getting restless. People are coming onto the field, shouting things I can't understand. Those who were fighting turn toward the newcomers.

"We may not have won this yet," I say. "We have to convince all these people."

Cynthia steps forward. She puts a bright-yellow spell to her throat. "Citizens"—her voice booms across the field—"the Grand Chancellor is dead. Everyone has their freedom from him."

Cheers sound throughout the crowd. More than I expected and hoped for. The people are just as glad to be done with him as we are. There are certain to be his supporters still around, but none of them make themselves known.

Cynthia stops the spell and grins at me. "We've won."

It's true. After spending my life under the rule of my father, and recently the Grand Chancellor, not only am I free, but so is every other person in Chardonia.

* * *

"WHAT EXACTLY HAPPENED?" I ask as we sit in a tent on the tournament grounds, Nathaniel's arm around me.

They take turns telling me what happened from their point of view. It leaves me feeling somehow bigger than I actually am. That I did something better than ever. I guess I did. It's not every day you defeat the evil leader of a country. Not every day you almost die to kill him.

"I suppose I owe my life to you," I say to Waverly.

"No." She shakes her head, eyes glistening. "We all owe our lives and our future happiness to you."

I'm overcome by her words. It's difficult to speak past the tightening in my throat. "I just did my best when the opportunity presented itself. Like any of you would have done."

"You did more than that," Serena says. "You defeated the Grand Chancellor. We all owe you our lives and happiness."

I blush. "Are Zade and Daniel all right?" I ask.

Serena drops her gaze.

"They will be," Cynthia says. "Eventually."

"Where are they?"

"They're being seen to by a healer," Cynthia says.

"Why don't you go to him?" I ask Serena. "I'm fine now. I'll see you soon."

She nods and jumps to her feet like she can't wait to be with the man she loves. "I'll be back to see you soon." With that, she's quickly out of the tent.

I swallow past the thickening in my throat. "I hope they can heal. I know they're both strong."

"If the Grand Chancellor wasn't already dead," Waverly says, "I'd make him pay for what he's done to them. But they will heal." Conviction fills her voice.

"You can join her," I say.

"They need some time alone, I'm sure. I'll see him soon enough." Though she does look at the tent opening like she wants to follow Serena out, she stays put.

"Where are we to go from here?" I ask.

"First we'll make certain nobody cruel like the Grand Chancellor steps up to lead," Cynthia says.

"Maybe you should lead," I tell her.

She looks startled by the thought, but after a moment her face calms. "Maybe I should."

"That would be a definite improvement," Waverly says.

"We'll see what the people want, but I think I'd like to, if they are interested in having me."

"Most of them are already eating out of the palm of your hands," I say. "The only ones who aren't are the Grand Chancellor's followers. There shouldn't be many of them left."

"It'll take time to know for certain," Cynthia says. "But I think there are going to be a few law officers."

"What happened to them?" I ask.

"They ran off the moment you pulled out the gun," Cynthia says.

A thought suddenly hits me and guilt overcomes me. "Where is Tawny? Is she all right? She was supposed to give me the noncalifrasum, but she didn't show up. I was worried about what might have happened to her."

"I got a note from her earlier," Waverly says. "She's alive and well, trying to help the tarnished at the Grand Chancellor's house. Apparently she couldn't convince your guards she was the one who needed to deliver the califrasum, so she switched it with the fake stuff when they weren't looking."

Relief fills me at the news. Without her, I would have never been able to shoot the Grand Chancellor and end this whole life-long nightmare. "How did she get a note out?"

"The spells all went down around the Grand Chancellor's house when he died."

"There's one thing I'm curious about," Waverly says. "If you're up for trying it, I'd like to know how much magic you have. I don't know if I got your magic back for you, or if I stole some of the Grand Chancellor's."

The thought makes me gag. I want nothing of his. "I can try a spell, if you'd like."

"That sounds like a good idea," Nathaniel says. "Why don't you just do a light spell, a simple measurement of your magic?"

I nod, nervous about what may happen. I call upon my magic, expecting the normal pull, only there's barely a tug at all. When I let out the spell, it's just a faint spark. Everyone looks at me expectantly, like I'll burst out with more any second now.

"That's all there is," I say, uncertain whether that's good or bad. At least I don't have the Grand Chancellor's power.

"I'm sorry I didn't get your magic back," Waverly says.

"It's fine. I managed without it most of my life; I can manage now. Besides, I would have hated ending up with the Grand Chancellor's magic. No one should have that type of power."

I yawn, overcome by exhaustion. The tiny spell wore me out more than I thought it would. I have a hard time just holding my head up.

"I think we'd best let you rest," Waverly says.

"Perhaps. But I'm eager to get up and get things settled. I want to go home, truth be told, but we don't have a home to go to, and I don't want to go back to the Grand Chancellor's."

"We can use one of the safe houses until we find something," Waverly says.

I sigh with contentment. Find something, we will. And it will be all ours.

Waverly

CHAPTER 63

A week has passed since that fateful day at the tournament. I can't help but think things could have gone so much differently. But they didn't. Bethany prevailed. And here I am, assisting the Chardonians clean up their lives. This is much more enjoyable than helping them fight a war. I love aiding the people in a more peaceful way.

The power plants have all been taken down. Healing centers have been set up with the cooperation of those from Envado and Chryos. I suspect the Chryons only assist because they want to trade with Chardonians again, but right now we'll take all the help we can get.

It will be a while before Chardonia is at a point to trade again —many pieces still need to be picked up—but I have faith it will happen. There won't be power to the country for a while, but it will be worth it. For now, the people are healing.

Arms warp around me from behind. I squeal and turn around to find Jack with a grin on his face.

"You surprised me." I lean forward and kiss his cheek.

"A good surprise, I hope."

"The best."

"Are we going to see your brother now?"

My happiness is hampered a little. It's not every day one is stronger than their big brother. I hope that soon changes. "Yes. I've missed him too much to skip a daily visit.

It only takes us ten minutes on horseback to reach the house he's staying at with Lukas and a few other men from Envado. I will never get in a carriage again as long as I can help it.

We enter the house, and I go straight for Zade's room. He's sitting in a chair when we get there, Serena sitting right beside them. The two have been inseparable since his return.

Zade is looking better. With the help of magic, his bruises are all gone. He's still thin but putting on a little weight. I have a feeling the longest thing to heal will be his mind. He doesn't talk about his experience a great deal, but what he does say chills me to my toes.

"Waverly, how good to see you," he says, getting to his feet. It's his usual greeting to me now.

I wrap him in a hug. "I've missed you."

"Well, we're together now."

We both take a seat, Jack sitting beside me. "How are things going?"

"We have news." A rare smile creeps to Zade's face.

"What news is this?" Though I think I already know.

"We're finally going to be married, as soon as your parents arrive," Serena says.

"Congratulations. We're so happy for you. I can't wait for the event," I say.

"Me either." Zade's still smiling. "Father thinks he's doing well enough to come soon. We shouldn't have to wait much longer."

"Good. You both deserve to be together."

We chat a little more before leaving so he can get the rest he needs. Jack joins me on a horse ride, both of us reveling in the freedom.

"We should do this more often," I say. "At least three times every day."

He laughs. "There's not enough time for that in a day. Not with everything we have to continue rebuilding."

"True," I say with a sigh. "We're well on our way, though. I hope Cynthia is elected to the new council."

"Oh, I think she'll do just fine. Especially with women allowed to vote."

He brings his horse close to mine until they're touching, and he leans in for a kiss. I lean in as well, heat filling me as our lips meet. Everything we ever could want is ours.

Cynthia

CHAPTER 64

True to the talk directly after Bethany defeated the Grand Chancellor, I'm happily working my way into the government. Lukas is beside me the entire time, supporting me. Others want to join as well. Some, like Daniel, I'm excited about. Others, like previous law officers who still resent women and don't want me around at all, I want to smash out.

We're holding an election for government officials. It's almost time to find out if I made it or not, and I'm all eagerness to find out.

"What if I don't make it?" I say.

"You'll make it," Lukas says. "If not, we'll have a lot more time for kissing."

I blush. "Lukas!"

"What? It's true."

I blush harder.

Serena, Waverly, and Bethany hurry over. "They're about to announce the winners."

Nervous energy flows through me. I have to work to make certain it doesn't come out as a spell. "Maybe I should plug my ears until it's all over."

Waverly gently knocks my shoulder. "No need for that. They'll call your name; don't you worry about it."

"What if they don't?"

"Then you'll find another way to help out," Bethany says. "We all know you have it in you. You'll make something wonderful, whatever you do."

A woman I don't recognize steps up to the platform on the old tournament field. Just having a woman announce the winners says something. This country is changing for the better already.

"The person taking the head of the council as the head councilman is Cynthia."

The crowd cheers. I feel as if I'm suddenly in a dream world. How can this really be me? How can it not? They called my name. *I won.* I'll not only be able to help the people, but I'll be in charge of the council, making sure it runs correctly.

Lukas nudges me. "Congratulations. Now get up there. They're all waiting for you."

I realize it's true. While the crowd still cheers, the woman at the platform looks at me expectantly. Before I go, I give Lukas a firm kiss on the lips, and I give each of my sisters and Waverly a hug. This is really happening. It's happening. I'm going to help the people. Something I would have never expected even six months ago.

I make my way across the field and onto the platform. The woman finishes announcing the council members, one of whom is Daniel. The only member of the new council that was on the previous one. He should be able to offer some interesting insight.

The woman turns to me and says in a voice the crowd can't hear, "I think they would like some words from you."

I nod, though my hands are shaking. I spell my voice to be loud enough to be heard far across the field. "Thank you all, for electing me to lead over you. I promise I will do the best job I can. No matter what, I will work hard to ensure both men and women have equal rights."

The crowd cheers. Their shouts are so wild, I feel like I don't need to say anything further. These are a people excited to find freedom in their new life. And I'm excited to help them find it. Freedom is ours.

Serena

CHAPTER 65

Finally, it's wedding time. I've waited too long for this day. At last it's here. I can't wait to see my soon-to-be husband, Zade. Though I just saw him last night, I ache to lay eyes on him again. After losing him for so long to the Grand Chancellor's dungeon and spending months fearing for his health and safety, only to find all my worst fears were true, the only thing I want to do is look at him and hold his hand. To simply be with him and never let go.

But it's time. We can move on past that stage in our lives, and everyone we care about is here to witness it. Zade's father is finally well enough to travel along with his mother. I met them yesterday, to find I will love my in-laws. It will be a nice change from my own parents, though mother is getting along with me better now than ever before.

Mother is here too. She's got all the kids in tow. I'd like to think things will be easier for her now, but she still seems to be having a hard time adjusting. Especially to Bethany, who still bears the marks of being tarnished, bald and tattooed, though her tattoos are no longer spelled to glow, like they were when the

Grand Chancellor ruled. She's sitting next to Nathaniel, who is surprisingly gentle with her. Exactly what she needs.

Next to them are Waverly and Jack. The two of them tease each other mercilessly. I've never seen a relationship like theirs before. Then again, I've seen few healthy relationships. But that's changing. Cynthia and Lukas are just as endearing, if not as teasing. I have a feeling my wedding will be the first of many.

And of course, Katherine is here. She made my wedding dress. It's a deep, form-fitting, red with a small train. A simple black bow tied around my waist makes my hair look darker. Only she could pull off something so glorious and tasteful. She's here with her husband, Charles. The two of them make almost as perfect as a couple as Zade and I do.

It's then I spot him, smiling like he's just won the best prize ever, but he's looking right at me. I smile back, thinking how lucky it was all those years ago that he won me in the tournament. The only right thing that happened in my former life. And now we're about to be together forever. Nothing will ever come between us again. Well, except maybe the usual bickering between husband and wife his mother warned me about. Smart woman. I think there's a lot for me to learn from her.

As I walk closer to him, Zade's cheeks redden. I hope he never grows out of blushing. As soon as I reach him, I lean into him, letting him wrap his arms around me while I wrap mine around him. I don't even care there's a whole audience here to watch us. I just want to be with him. To find freedom in our new life together.

Peace settles over me. I know there are lots of changes to come. Lots of work that still needs to be done and things I need to learn. But for here and now, I feel confident this is what's supposed to be, my loved ones all gathered around in celebration.

So much has already changed, and more will change. I'm confident it will be for the better. There's a whole people out there I want to help guide in my own way. I want everyone to know, no matter who they are, everyone can have what's become ours.

Bethany

CHAPTER 66

Five Years Later

I TAKE a hold of Abby's hand. She's five and a half, and her hand fits perfectly in mine. I can't imagine a better thing to do at this moment than go on a walk with my littlest sister. She holds on to me as she jabbers away, completely trusting. I love all my sisters, but Abby and I have a special bond.

Nathaniel acts as any good husband would, clearing away the rocks and branches so we'll have a soft spot to picnic. He looks up at me with a grin. I smile back. Though we'll never have kids of our own, and I'll always be bald and tattooed, he never seems to mind.

There are lots of tarnished boys who need care. We spend a lot of time with them when Nathaniel isn't helping to fix all the problems his father's rule created. Even though it's been five years, there are still scars left among the people. Having Nathaniel help with them gives us both a sense of peace.

Serena comes toward us, glowing, her belly big with child. Her second. Zade carries littler Serenity on his shoulders, looking much the same as I remember when I first met him, though perhaps a little more aged in the eyes and with a limp that will never go away.

I don't know everything he and Serena have gone through after his imprisonment in the Grand Chancellor's dungeon, but I know it hasn't been easy for either of them. They finally seem to be growing past that now.

"Is Cynthia still coming?" I ask when Serena gets to me.

"You know how she is. Always busy now. I'm sure Lukas will drag her along soon enough."

Waverly appears next, a babe in her arms and Jack at her side. I still marvel at how the two have gotten along. Waverly has never had any desire to return to her home country, other than for visits. She claims her place is here now. With her husband and child.

She runs a charity for women, helping them find their new place in society. Maybe even more than that, helping them discover who they really can be. Despite the years that have gone by, the pain isn't easily erased. She's doing much to help with that.

When Waverly and Jack reach us, Jack spreads out a blanket across the ground Nathaniel has cleared. We all settle on it, Abby going from baby to baby until she finally settles on chatting away to Serenity.

A moment later, Lukas appears with Cynthia at his side. She's head of the council still, though she says this is her last year as such. After this, she plans on helping with the government in other ways. The people don't need another leader who never steps down from office, she thinks. I agree, though she's done a fabulous job of not just putting the country back together, but restoring relationships with other countries as well.

"Sorry we're late," she says.

"We planned on it starting now," Serena says. "We just told you earlier, so you'd be on time."

Cynthia laughs. "You know me well."

As we get our picnic underway, I can't help but think how much has changed over the years. How much happier we all are. Not just my family, but the nation as a whole.

No matter who one is, everyone can have what's become mine.

AFTERWORD

If you enjoyed reading this book, please consider helping the author by leaving a review where you purchased the book and/or on Goodreads.

You can sign up to receive newsletters from Janeal Falor at www.janealfalor.com on the contact or books page and receive a free book. Or contact the author directly at janealfalor@gmail.com

ACKNOWLEDGMENTS

This series has been an amazing journey. I hope you've enjoyed Serena, Katherine, Cynthia, Waverly, and Bethany's story as much as I enjoyed writing them. These girls have become dear to my heart. Though they are fictional, I've had people tell me how their lives emulate these sweet girls. My heart goes out to all of you. I hope you can fight your battles bravely, no matter what they may be.

My sister, Karen C. Eddington, is not only a funny, amazing person, but knows when to give me critical feedback. I appreciate all your help making this series what it is. Lori Hall, thank you for always being my friend, listening ear, and idea bouncer. I know this series would never have happened if it wasn't for you.

Thank you Sotia Lazu for being such a fantastic editor. Reading your side notes always makes the edits worth doing. I love to see you cheer for my characters or being sad when something bad is about to happed. Girl, you rock! Thank you Sharon Umbaugh for helping me find what I was missing and cleaning things up.

A huge thank you to Rebecca Webb for being my friend and

taking an interest in my writing. Your words of encouragement mean more than I can say.

Many thanks to my dear Tai, Xandria, and Will. May you know that mommy loves you dearly even when she's going crazy in her fictional world.

To my husband, Erik. I love you more than words can say. You are the most swoon worthy computer geek ever, and my life as a writer would be much more stressful without you. Between backups and help when I can get formatting right, you're always there for me. You are mine forever, and I am yours.

Thank you, my dear readers. You are The Best.

ABOUT THE AUTHOR

Amazon best selling author Janeal Falor lives in Utah with her husband and three children. In her non-writing time she teaches her kids to make silly faces, cooks whatever strikes her fancy, and attempts to cultivate a garden even when half the things she plants die. When it's time for a break she can be found taking a scenic drive with her family, fencing, or drinking hot chocolate.